From what she'd seen of Ryan, Sabrina was pretty certain he was the man she wanted.

But she also had a feeling this "wild ride" equaled a plate of poison food to a starving man—pleasure with a lethal endgame. Jumping out of a plane was enough of a dare, thank you very much. She didn't need to add a hot cowboy with a rock-hard body and sultry brown, bedroom eyes. Besides, it wasn't as if she was champing at the bit to skydive anyway.

"I can wait for the other instructor," she said. "No rush, really. I'll come back next weekend, or maybe the one after that."

A slow smile charged Ryan's too-handsome face. "I'll be easy with you, darlin'. I promise."

He promises. Said the cat to the mouse, she thought cynically, but that didn't stop her imagination from conjuring an image of her strapped to a parachute, with him attached to her...er...backside. Uh-huh, he would be dangerous in all kinds of ways.

Blaze™

Dear Reader,

The sun isn't all that sizzles in Texas since three ex-Army Special Forces buddies, once members of the elite "Crazy Aces" team, opened the skydiving operation, The Texas Hotzone. In *Jump Start,* you met Bobby Evans, who was determined to seduce the love of his life back into his bed, where he planned to win her heart. Now, it's time to get *High Octane,* with Ryan "Cowboy" Walker, a man with nothing to lose. And one of the things I absolutely loved about writing Ryan's story is that he never, ever, backs down from a dare.

So when Ryan meets Sabrina Cameron, the prim and proper journalist who needs a little fun and excitement in her life but isn't sure *she dares,* Ryan is all about making sure she does—with him. Only, before Ryan knows what hits him, Sabrina turns the tables, and Ryan isn't sure who's challenging whom. With each hot little encounter he shares with her, Sabrina leads Ryan to the one ultimate dare he swore he would never take—the one called love.

So read onward for a wild and wicked *High Octane* ride—I dare you. And so does Ryan!

Lisa Renee Jones

Lisa Renee Jones

HIGH OCTANE

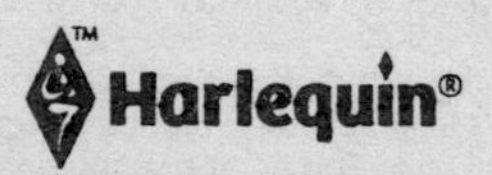

TORONTO NEW YORK LONDON
AMSTERDAM PARIS SYDNEY HAMBURG
STOCKHOLM ATHENS TOKYO MILAN MADRID
PRAGUE WARSAW BUDAPEST AUCKLAND

ISBN-13: 978-0-373-79605-2

HIGH OCTANE

This edition published by arrangement with Harlequin Books S.A.

For questions and comments about the quality of this book please contact us at Customer_eCare@Harlequin.ca.

www.eHarlequin.com

Printed in U.S.A.

ABOUT THE AUTHOR

Lisa spends her days writing the dreams playing in her head. Before becoming a writer, Lisa lived the life of a corporate executive, often taking the red-eye flight out of town and flying home for the excitement of a Little League baseball game. Visit Lisa at www.lisareneejones.com.

Books by Lisa Renee Jones

HARLEQUIN BLAZE

339—HARD AND FAST
442—LONE STAR SURRENDER
559—HOT TARGET
590—JUMP START

HARLEQUIN NOCTURNE

THE BEAST WITHIN
BEAST OF DESIRE
BEAST OF DARKNESS

To my home state of Texas, where the Margaritas are chilled, the fajitas are sizzling, and the cowboys are just plain hot. And to all my friends and family in Austin—Hook 'em Horns. I love ya'll.

1

"SABRINA! WHERE IS SABRINA?"

With disbelief, Sabrina Cameron stepped out of the ladies' room of the *Austin Herald* to hear her name shouted in the distinctive gravelly tones of new editor-in-chief, Frank Roberts.

Only a month before, she'd said goodbye to New York City, and her U.S. Senator father, along with a high-profile political column at a renowned newspaper. So much for thinking she'd left behind the hectic life where being hunted down in the restroom was the norm.

"Sabrina!" came another shout, as Frank barreled around the corner and into the hallway, his tall, lanky frame in pursuit of his target—her. The man was high-strung, with a penchant for long hours filled with hectic demands, usually made by him of everyone else.

His hard, gray eyes narrowed as he took in her appearance. Surprise flickered in his keen stare as he noted her long, brunette hair, worn loose now for the first time since her arrival, and then her unusually casual attire: a pale-blue Western shirt tucked into her black jeans.

Lips thinning disapprovingly, he demanded, "Why are you dressed like that? Where's the suit you had on this morning?"

"I'm reporting from the Kyle Strawberry Festival this afternoon," she said, looking forward to a fun night without the pressure of having anyone analyzing her political views versus those of her father. Oh, and the cowboys. She was really liking the combo of tight Wranglers with scuffed boots that the men wore like business suits here in Texas. You never knew what was under those Wranglers—a millionaire or a ranch hand—and no one seemed to care. It was refreshing. And sexy.

"Put the other outfit back on," Frank ordered brusquely, snapping her out of her momentary Wrangler fixation. "You're going downtown for a press conference with the mayor."

"Oh, no," Sabrina insisted, "that's not my area. I don't do politics. Not anymore." Nor did she want anyone to know she ever had. So much so that she'd taken a pseudonym to ensure no one would connect her with her past. She needed her own life, her own identity, an ability to make decisions without becoming manipulated by how they might impact her father's career.

"I need you on this," he said, his arms folding in front of him. "You're going."

"No politics," she repeated, shoving her fists to her hips. "That was a condition of my employment."

"I've given you a fifth-grade 'Dare' graduation, a 5k

run, and now apparently a silly strawberry festival," he bellowed. "Now *you're* giving me this. You need to get your backside to that press conference and *not* in those jeans."

"You gave me those stories because that's what we agreed I'd do the first six months," she said, her voice low as she quickly made sure no one else was around before continuing. "Fluff stories that establish me as someone other than who I was back in New York. Stories that keep me off the radar. I moved across country to make a new life for myself. A press conference with the mayor is not a good enough reason for me to risk jeopardizing that."

"Then I guess you didn't hear that an American soldier, one of our own, robbed a bank last night, and he was connected to a drug cartel. That's big news. The right take on the story could get you a television mention, or maybe even an interview."

"I heard," she said. "People do stupid stuff every day. It's sad but it doesn't require me to report on it personally. And you aren't going to use me to get your own press. The last thing I want is a television mention that will destroy the entire reason I'm here—to get away from the pressure of the spotlight."

"You know that world," he said. "You can find out what I want to know."

"'That world'?" she said. "You mean politics? Yes. I do. And I wish I didn't. Exactly why I came here and took a job with specific duties that do not include 'that world.'" She was thirty-two, long past having every breath she took approved by her father.

"What if I told you I have a person on the mayor's staff who says the mayor not only knows this soldier, but he's trying to bury this story."

"Why would he do that?" she asked, before she could stop herself.

"Maybe the mayor is dirty and I know how you hate a dirty politician," he said. "Maybe he's even involved with the drug cartel. The possibilities are endless. That's why I need an expert on this story. Do I have your attention now?"

"No," she lied. "No, you do not." She'd come here to create a new life, not move the old one to another state. "This isn't why you hired me. And you know my father is known to be highly ambitious and that he's rising as a leader for his party. I don't need to be in the middle of a scandal involving a Governor. Especially not one of the opposing party, which this one is."

"If anyone can get inside this story—"

"I don't want inside this story," she said, cutting him off.

"Well, I do," he said. "And that means you do. This is investigative reporting, Sabrina. Not political-opinion commentating. It's about facts. And no one can judge you for the truth."

"My job—"

"Is to do what I tell you to do," he said. "And mine is to report the news by using every resource possible. Strawberry festivals are beneath you. Period. The end."

His eyes sharpened, his voice firmed. "The press conference is at four o'clock. Be there."

She ground her teeth, fighting the part of her that yearned for more substantive reporting, the part she'd dismissed to get her life back. She liked plans. And this story didn't fit her plan.

"Sabrina," he said.

"Oh, all right, Frank," she said. "I'll go, but I don't want my name attached. Have someone else write the story with my notes."

His lips twitched and he turned with a mumbled, "We'll talk," and headed toward the newsroom.

Sabrina debated pursuit and that "talk" right now, but Jennifer Jones, the petite blonde veterinarian who was the newly established pet-advice columnist appeared in her path, rushing toward her.

"What the heck was he shouting your name for?" She stopped in front of Sabrina. "I swear I'll never get used to this place. I need to get back to my clinic. Barking dogs and hissing cats are so much nicer than hot tempers and demanding bellows."

Sabrina might have laughed at the flustered look on Jenn's face, if not for the knots in her own stomach. "Can I go with you?"

"Depends," Jennifer said, smiling. "How do you feel about chickens? I hear I have someone bringing one in this afternoon."

"A chicken?" Sabrina asked, laughing. It had only been a month, but she already considered Jennifer a friend. The woman and her silly animal stories hit all the right notes at all the right times. "You can't be serious."

"As a mama hen," she said. "This is Texas. People take their chickens seriously. This one belongs to a high-school kid in Future Farmers of America."

"In New York," Sabrina told her, "it's the rats we take seriously, only they aren't school projects or pets."

Jennifer snorted. "And here I thought New York City didn't have wildlife." She smiled. "Did Frank's shout mean you are otherwise occupied or can you grab some lunch before I retreat to the animal kingdom of my clinic?"

Sabrina blew hair from her eyes. "It means I need a margarita and some chocolate, though I'll settle for lunch and dessert. But I need to—"

"Drive," Jennifer said for her. "I know."

Sabrina frowned. "You do?"

She nodded. "We've been to lunch three times, and every time you found a reason to drive. Just like you have to fill your coffee cup to an exact spot. You're a control freak."

Sabrina opened her mouth to deny this, but Jennifer held up a finger. "Let me go grab my purse." Jennifer rushed away toward the newsroom in a flash of long blond hair and bubbly personality.

Sabrina stood absolutely still, frowning over Jennifer's assessment that she was a control freak. She wasn't a control freak. Her father was. And she intended to prove that fact to Jennifer over lunch.

An hour later, seated in a red-leather booth of a

family-style restaurant, the main course completed, Sabrina helped herself to the huge brownie, covered with chocolate and ice cream, in front of her.

"I'm not a control freak," Sabrina insisted, having just taken Jennifer into her confidence with a confession of how and why she'd come to Texas.

Jennifer arched a brow.

Sabrina pursed her lips in rejection of that silent challenge. Darn this woman for seeing so much, for forcing her to face facts. "Fine. I admit it. I'm a control freak, but it has been by necessity. Back home, every step I took was analyzed, dissected for political gain. I'm out of that environment now, and I want to be free, but it's hard."

Silence followed as Jennifer savored a big bite of brownie, and then said, "Have you ever watched the *Dog Whisperer*?"

Sabrina laughed in disbelief at the off-the-wall comment that seemed to fit nowhere in this conversation. "Big Fan," Sabrina admitted. "And not because I'm trying to be a dog whisperer. I don't even have a dog. It's the way those animals instantly submit, well...*that* kind of control is really sexy."

Jennifer set her spoon down. "Listen, this isn't going where I meant for it to go. We are talking about giving away control, not making it sexy."

"Oh, good grief," Sabrina said in realization of her mixup. "I'm completely conflicted. I'm in way worse shape than I thought." And on that note, she did the only logical thing she could do—she took a huge bite of her brownie.

"We're all confused," Jennifer assured her, but not before she stifled a laugh. "It's called being human."

"Then maybe you have the right idea," Sabrina said. "Spend all your time with animals." She frowned. "Oh, wait. You're married, though, right?"

"I'm married, yes," Jennifer said and wiggled an eyebrow. "And thankfully Bobby knows all the right times to be an animal." They shared a laugh, and then she continued, "What I was going to say is this. In the *Dog Whisperer*, when a dog is aggressive, Cesar shows people how to make that animal become submissive. He has the animal lie on its side in the middle of other dominants—to learn to accept a submissive position."

"Okay," Sabrina said. "Just for the record, I know you're a vet so I'm not going to be offended by you comparing me to a dog. But I still don't get the point."

"The point is that he conditions the dogs to see that less aggressive behavior gets them what they want, which in their case is praise," she said. "I think you need to condition yourself to let go of control, so you can see that the world won't shatter because you do." Her eyes lit up. "And I know just how you can do it."

"If it involves a chicken, I can tell you right now, I want no part of it."

"Skydiving," Jennifer said. "It's perfect."

Sabrina gaped. "Skydiving." That was the last thing she'd expected to hear. "Are you crazy? You want me to jump out of a plane? Surely you can think of something less dramatic?"

"Bobby and a few of his Army pals own Texas Hotzone, a skydiving operation thirty minutes outside of Austin. You can make your first jump with Caleb. He's one of Bobby's best friends. A nice, soft-spoken guy who's gentle. You can give him control without feeling like you really gave it away, and he'll keep you safe."

"No," Sabrina replied, setting her spoon down in rejection. "The idea behind me moving here was to live life. In other words—I don't have a death wish."

Jennifer shrugged. "I jump and I love it. But then, I'm not a control freak. I guess that allows me to enjoy things you can't."

"Oh, that was a low blow," Sabrina chided, narrowing her eyes on her friend. "Really low."

"I know." She leaned in close. "But it worked and you know it." Her watch beeped. "Shoot. I need to go." She reached for her purse. "I won't be back to the paper until next week." She set a business card on the table. "That's the address of Texas Hotzone. Meet me there on Saturday before two. That gives you three days to chicken out, but don't do it. You moved across the country to change your life, so change it. Don't relocate the old one." She pushed to her feet. "I dare you."

Sabrina sat watching Jennifer depart without really seeing her. She'd moved across country, left her job, changed her name, and all for what? To remain captive to her father's world?

She grimaced. Who was she kidding? She didn't

want to report on strawberry festivals. It was simply that strawberry festivals were safe. Frank had been right. Reporting facts was different from writing her political POV as she had in New York. And investigative reporting had been her roots, the way she'd started in the media years before.

She *wanted* to go to this press conference. She wanted to find out the facts. She wanted to write the story she wanted to write. To choose the friends she wanted to choose. To choose a man because he was exciting, not safe, either.

Heck, she wanted to be able to have a one-night stand if she so desired and not worry about being gossip fodder. But she'd never dared such a thing before. She gave that a moment's consideration, picturing a set of rock-hard abs, perfect pecs and wild, erotic passion.

She sighed and discarded the idea, inhaling a spoonful of her half-eaten dessert and deciding to savor every bite. The brownie was the closest thing to orgasm she was going to get anytime soon. Maybe she'd better go with skydiving. At least jumping out of a plane came without the risk of scandal. The risk of scandal... Would she ever be free?

IT WAS SATURDAY AFTERNOON, a hot time at the Hotzone for Ryan "Cowboy" Walker, who sauntered behind the front desk to complete the day's log. He was outta here early today, taking off for the first time in a month, since their grand opening. He was heading out for an appointment with a real-estate agent to look at houses, though he hadn't shared that little detail with anyone. He'd given himself a deadline for deciding if he was committed to the civilian life, and once he committed, he would be fully committed. Though secretly the idea of owning a home scared the crap out of him, far more than any of the many snake-infested jungles he'd seen in his time. The only home he'd ever been willing to claim was the Army, with his AK-14 as his front door.

Ryan believed you did things all the way or not at all. People who walked a line usually ended up dead or miserable. He didn't like either of those choices. Which was why he'd left the Army a month before and invested with several of his Crazy Aces in thc Hotzone. At one time, he would have sworn he'd have been a life-timer. But soldiers followed orders without question, and he no longer could. Not when he'd come to realize there was an outside agency involved in their mission, of questionable ethics. Nothing had been what it seemed. And so here he was, about to house-hunt, forced into domestication like some sort of wild cat, but still committed.

He slammed the logbook shut, satisfied he was ready for Monday's jump class. He was going to show the new Special Forces recruits what had put the Crazy in the Aces—namely, him. They'd never jump out of a plane with anything but cool confidence when he was done scaring the hell out of them. Better they wet their training pants on his clock than on the enemies'.

Ryan was headed around the counter and toward the door when his gaze caught on the parking lot and the woman approaching the building; she gave *hot* a whole new meaning. He stopped dead in his tracks and a low whistle escaped his lips.

With an all-consuming interest that made house-hunting a distant memory, he tracked the curvy brunette's path.

His gaze simmered on the confident stride of the woman headed his way, those long legs eating the distance between them. Oh, yeah. He was going to like this woman. Anticipation charged his nerve-endings with a fire he'd not known in far too long. His around-the-clock work schedule had left no time for dating or other pleasures. A dry spell that would soon be ending, he decided. His groin tightened at the sight of the sexy she-devil's snug black jeans and fitted black T-shirt, both of which hugged her with deliciously arousing perfection.

She reached for the door; her silky dark hair fluttered around petite shoulders and high breasts. He wanted that hair on his face, on his stomach. He wanted this woman.

She stepped inside the small office equipped with a couple of steel desks and not much more, shoving her sunglasses on top of her head as the door swung shut behind her. Light green eyes the color of new grass blinked him into focus and connected with his, the attraction between them instant, hot. No. *Damn* hot. Electricity charged the air, stroking his cock to full attention, the room so silent it was eerie.

"Hi," she said in a rich-wine kind of voice that rippled along his nerve-endings and sent a rush of fire straight through his veins.

His gaze slid to the rise and fall of her ample breasts, and then lifted in time to see the alluring scrape of teeth along her full red bottom lip. He wanted to taste her. He wanted to taste all of her. Ryan tipped his cowboy hat, undisguised interest in the heated look he fixed in her direction.

Another silent, crackling moment followed before she announced, "I'm here to see Caleb."

Ryan barely contained a curse. Caleb. She was here to see Caleb. His partner. His fellow Ace. His friend. Ryan ground his teeth at the off-limits territory he was treading on, an out-of-character possessiveness rising within him. He'd never taken anything from one of the Aces. They were family, his blood without blood. But Caleb had better stake his claim on this woman and stake it fast. Because Ryan wanted her in a bad way, and what Ryan Walker wanted, Ryan Walker went after, and blood was the only thing that could stop him.

2

RYAN WAS LOCKED on to the brunette beauty, not about to let her get past him without getting what he wanted, and that was a whole lot more than name, rank and serial number. That was, until she was intercepted.

"Sabrina!" Jennifer shouted, charging past him and into the path of his target. "You're late," she accused, chiding the woman who'd become the center of his attention. "I thought you weren't coming."

"You mean you thought I was a big ol' chicken," replied the woman, Sabrina. She followed the response with a laugh. It was a sexy, smoky sound that did nothing to take the edge off Ryan's growing desire or the bulge beneath his zipper.

Jennifer's hands went to her hips, her back to Ryan, her body irritatingly blocking his view of Sabrina. "We both know your tardiness means you almost pulled a no-show."

Jennifer stepped a bit to her right, her arms still planted on those hips, and Ryan could see the flush spread across Sabrina's ivory-perfect skin before she asked, "Was there a specific time I was supposed to be here? I thought you said Saturday…as in anytime today."

"Don't play coy with me," Jennifer scolded instantly. "I said before two o'clock and you know it."

Sabrina laughed, skipping any attempt at denial. "Okay, I almost talked myself out of coming," she admitted. "I know I'm late."

"Ah-huh," Jennifer said. "That's what I thought. And you secretly hoped it would be too late to jump. Well, you got your wish. Caleb is booked all afternoon."

Ryan leaned one elbow on the counter and crossed his dusty, booted feet. To hell with house-hunting. "I'll take her up," he said in a lazy drawl that defied the outright molten heat charging through his body.

Sabrina glanced around Jennifer, her pale green eyes glinting like crystals as they slid down his body in a long, lingering inspection, before her gaze popped to his. "And you would be?" she inquired.

"A better choice than Caleb," he assured her.

"Not for Sabrina," Jennifer countered and gave him her back. "Ryan is a wild ride you don't want any part of. Trust me. You want Caleb."

FROM WHAT SHE'D SEEN of Ryan, Sabrina was pretty certain he was the man she wanted. But she also had a feeling this "wild ride" equaled a plate of poisoned food to a starving man—pleasure with a lethal endgame. Jumping out of a plane was enough of a dare, thank you very much. She didn't need to add a hot cowboy with a rock-hard body and sultry, brown, bedroom eyes. Besides, it wasn't as if she was chomping at the bit to jump to her death anyway.

"I can wait for Caleb," she said. "No rush, anyway. I can always come back next weekend."

A slow smile filled Ryan's too-handsome face. "I'll be easy with you, darlin'. I promise."

He promises. Said the cat to the mouse, she thought cynically, but that didn't stop her imagination from conjuring an image of her strapped to a parachute, with his front attached to her…er…backside. Oh, yeah, he was dangerous. In all kinds of ways.

"No, Ryan," Jennifer said urgently, and shifted her attention to Sabrina. "Caleb is calm and controlled. He'll be a pillar if you get scared."

"I'm calm and controlled," Ryan said.

Jennifer took a long glance at Ryan. "There is a reason you take up the experienced jumpers, and you know it."

"Yeah," he agreed. "Because I teach them that calm control doesn't have to be boring. I push them to the edge rather than pull them back. I show them how to expand their limits."

The words resonated through Sabrina and spoke to her deep beneath the surface. She already knew how to be calm and controlled. She'd spent a lifetime living just that. What she didn't know how to do was be calm, controlled and daring at the same time. To live outside her safety zone. Ryan was more than the man she wanted. Ryan was the man she needed. "I'll jump with Ryan."

Jennifer started to object. "Sabrina—"

Sabrina gently touched her arm. "It's okay," she said in a low voice. "Really. I'm here, and honestly, if I leave, I may never do this. And it's a good idea. It's a good thing."

"You're sure?"

"Am I sure about jumping out of a plane?" Sabrina asked incredulously. "Of course not. But I can't go through hours of convincing myself to go through with this again. Now or never."

Jennifer looked as if she might argue and then grabbed Sabrina's hand. "This way."

Jennifer then tugged Sabrina toward the interior of the office. In her path stood Ryan, whom she passed with mere inches separating them. Ryan, who looked hotter and harder, upon closer inspection. And inspect she did, she lingered on his long, muscular thighs poured into tight denim that would no doubt be hugging her thighs in the very near future. Her mouth watered, and she jerked her attention upward, her gaze colliding with the only soft thing about Ryan—his brown eyes—the sizzle between them impossible to miss. She was, indeed, in for a wild ride, and amazingly, though she was scared, Sabrina realized something she couldn't ignore. She was excited. She felt alive for the first time in years. She was doing something she'd never have dreamed of doing a few months ago. She was changing her life, but also pushing herself to experience the world.

Unfortunately, the path to experiencing that world led—at least for the moment—away from Ryan and into what looked like a classroom. Sabrina soon found herself sitting at one of six steel folding tables, signing liability paperwork. Lots of it. Suddenly, she forgot long, hard Ryan and thought of the long, hard fall she might take if her chute didn't open.

"Okay," Jennifer said, sitting next to her. "Last signature." She pointed to the release form. "Sign here." But then she pulled the paper away. "Or don't. You can still change your mind."

Sabrina grabbed the paper and signed. "You are so not helping, Jennifer. Have you forgotten this was your idea?"

"It was my idea to send you up with Caleb," she said. "Not Ryan. Yes, he's part owner, yes, but that's not the point."

"Then what is?"

Jennifer let out a sigh and shifted in the steel chair. "I pushed you into this. I don't want you to have a bad experience. I want you to feel it was fun, and that it really did help you with the whole control-freak thing. And Caleb… he's sensitive, patient. He'll know if you've reached your limits. He'll know to pull you back. Ryan doesn't know limits. He'll push you. Especially if he knows why you're doing this."

"I can handle Ryan," Sabrina said. "And, truth be told, I have my reasons for choosing him."

"Jenn," came the deep, silky male voice, "call for you."

Sabrina's gaze lifted to directly across from them where Ryan filled the doorway with all kinds of hot male goodness, his hat tipped back, his sultry bedroom eyes fixed on her.

"Good luck, honey," Jennifer said. "You want him, he's all yours."

Ryan sauntered into the room, his dusty boots somehow only adding to his appeal as he gave Jennifer space to pass. Only she didn't pass. She paused. "Behave."

"Like a perfect angel," he assured her.

Jennifer snorted and disappeared.

Ryan leaned on the table directly in front of Sabrina. "Any hope one of those reasons for choosing me is my hot body?" His eyes twinkled with mischief.

Sabrina knew how to talk the talk. She was a politician's daughter, after all. "Actually, yes," she answered. "If you were out of shape and wheezing with every breath you drew, I can't say I'd be eager to jump out of a plane with you."

"I got the impression you weren't so eager to jump out of a plane with anyone."

"I'm sure a lot of people feel that way right about the time they sign their paperwork," Sabrina said.

"Only the ones who're talked into coming by someone else," he bantered. "But those people don't normally come alone. They come with a girlfriend, a boyfriend, a pal. That 'someone' they are trying to please by pushing themselves. Who are you here to please, Sabrina?"

Her chin lifted, fingers lacing together in front of

her, as they rested on top of the forms. "Myself." *For the first time in a very long time,* she added silently.

His eyes narrowed. "By pushing yourself to do something that scares you?"

"More like something I wouldn't normally do," she countered, not giving him more than she had to. This was her private journey. He didn't need to understand it to be a part of it.

"I need more than that if I'm taking you up," he said, rejecting her evasive answer.

"Why?" she snapped back instantly.

"Because I'm responsible for you up there," he said quickly, and then hit her with another question. "Are you afraid of heights?"

"No."

"Flying?"

"No."

"Falling?"

"No."

He studied her from under the ridge of his hat. "Dying?"

She considered that a moment. "No. No, I'm not afraid of dying. Once it's over, it's over. I think I'm okay with that. And do you ask these questions of everyone you take up for jumps?"

"No," he said. "But Caleb does."

"I didn't ask for Caleb," she said. "I asked for you."

"Why?"

Why. She'd walked right into that, but decided quickly she didn't care. Fine. He needed to know. He could know. Maybe sharing what she felt was a part of letting go of control. "Because I want to be pushed when I'm on the edge, not pulled back," she said, repeating what Jennifer had said when comparing the two men. "And because I know all about calm control, but I also know my limits are way too narrow." In other words, she wanted what he had offered.

A bit of surprise flickered across his face, followed by full-blown interest. "You really think you can handle me, Sabrina?"

Truth be told, he scared the holy bejeezus out of her, but he also excited her in a wickedly wonderful way she would never have dared to explore before now.

"I can handle you, cowboy," she assured him, with only a tiny white lie of uncertainty. "The question is... can you handle me?"

A slow smile slid onto his lips. "Sweetheart," he said, "if I can't, I'll die trying. And I'll do so a happy man."

He could have left out the *die,* considering they were about to jump out of a plane, but she managed to shove that aside, using the much-needed distraction of this hot man flirting with her.

Sabrina slid her paperwork forward. "I'm ready when you're ready."

Keeping his gaze locked on her face, he said, "You have a decision to make."

Wasn't jumping out of a plane with this man enough of a decision for one day? "Which is what?"

"First choice. You can take several hours of training

and jump on your own. That gives you the control, which appears to be important to you."

"Jumping out of a plane with no one anywhere near to help me is not what I call control," she said with no hesitation. In fact, she could feel her chest tightening, hear her heart pounding in her ears. "I thought I could jump with you? Can't I jump with you?" She pushed to her feet, and barely remembered doing it.

"Easy, sweetheart," he said softly, holding up his hands and slowly lowering them. "Of course you can jump with me. But maybe we should go get a beer instead of jumping out of a plane. Give you some time to think this through."

Suddenly, she realized how silly she must seem. My God. How had she become this scared little girl, too frightened to do what a million other people did without fear?

"No," she said, knowing that if she gave herself time to think, she'd back out. "Let's go. I want to jump."

Ryan stood up and walked around to her. Close. Towering over her. He extended his hand. "I'll make sure you enjoy every last minute."

3

SAFE, BORING, WITHOUT RISK. That described the men, and the events, of her life. She yearned for some excitement. She yearned to get past her fear. To live, to breathe, to enjoy life. Not just to survive it.

Sabrina stared at Ryan's hand—big, strong and an invitation to be daring that included so much more than jumping out of a plane. Her gaze lifted to his chocolate-brown stare, her hand tingling with the desire to touch him. The sexual tension between them was palpable, darn near consuming.

"Okay, Sabrina," Jennifer said, rushing into the room, "I have news that is either going to totally frustrate you, or make your day."

Sabrina turned to face her friend, abandoning Ryan's outstretched hand, as if her own hand were caught in the cookie jar. "News?" she asked.

Jennifer approached them and glanced suspiciously between Sabrina and Ryan. "What's going on?"

"Nothing," Sabrina said quickly and then shoved her

paperwork forward. "Nothing but paperwork, that is. All done."

"Paperwork," Ryan said dryly. "Nothing but paperwork. What's the news?"

With keen, skeptical eyes, Jennifer grabbed the forms, but focused on Ryan. "Apparently Marco Montey enjoyed himself yesterday. He's coming back this afternoon. He called jumping with you the best adrenaline rush he'd had off the track in years. In other words, you can't take Sabrina up today. And for the record…that a well-known daredevil views you as an adrenaline rush is a perfect example of why I don't want Sabrina with you." Her attention shifted apologetically to Sabrina. "Sorry, sweetie. I know it took a lot for you to get here today. I hate that I put you through this just to send you home, but maybe it's for the best."

Sabrina doubted Jennifer really understood how much it really had taken for her to get herself here. How much she'd fretted. How much she'd self-analyzed and denied. Not jumping? For the best? Sabrina wasn't so sure about that. No one should get this worked up for nothing. Yet, she had. Sighing, she squeezed her eyes shut. She should feel relieved she wasn't jumping. Instead, surprisingly, she felt let down.

Ryan cleared his throat, regaining their attention.

"Hang out until sunset, and I'll take you up then," Ryan offered, his brown eyes sympathetic rather than challenging. His words low, for her ears only. "If you're going to skydive once in your lifetime, that's the time to do it. It's truly one of the most spectacular sights ever."

Sabrina blinked, fighting the most unnerving urge to reach out and touch the light stubble on his ruggedly handsome face. The man loved skydiving. He lived life while she merely existed. She wished she could be brave and exciting like him, but the truth was, he was beyond her. And so was jumping out of a plane.

Swallowing regret that had everything to do with Ryan, and nothing to do with missing a chance to nose-dive from a plane, she replied, "I'd better pass because, you know, sitting here, waiting for my turn to jump from a plane, potentially to die, pretty much ruins the 'spectacular' part of the equation."

His lips twitched. "You aren't going to die. I promise."

She jumped on that—the only jump she intended to take now, no matter how tempting the man. "You can't promise that and you know it." He opened his mouth to respond, but she flung up a staying hand, her nostrils flaring with the spicy scent of him that darn near rattled her resolve. She forcefully added, "I like my promises absolute, not probably absolute. People die while skydiving."

"People die crossing the street," he countered.

"Rarely," she said.

"More frequently than they do jumping out of a plane."

"Because more people walk across streets, not because skydiving is safer. I checked the statistics. It's June, and already this year alone, there have been twenty-five people who've died in skydiving accidents. I spent all morning wondering if I would be number twenty-six. I can't sit here all afternoon and do the same." She shook her head. "No. I can't. I won't."

"Then let me worry," he said. "That's my job."

She snorted, and ran a hand through her hair. "In other words, neither of us will worry."

"And exactly what about that plan is bad?" he asked, the look on his face infuriatingly amused. And sexy. The man was sexy. Too sexy.

"Worry makes people careful," she stated. All her life she'd worried and headed off problems doing it.

"Worry makes people nervous, and then they make mistakes," he rebutted. "Training and experience make people aware, and awareness equals safety."

"Let it go, Ryan," Jennifer interjected. "It would be insane to make her wait. Montey has boatloads of money, and from what Bobby said, he doesn't mind spending it. He could be here all night. If he lives that long. I swear, Ryan…you'd better keep that man safe. If he dies here, we'll never get another client."

"Right. I'll make sure he dies someplace else. Check."

"Dang it, Ryan," Jennifer said. "You know what I mean. Montey is big news."

The haze of self-absorbed fear clearing, Sabrina asked, "Marco Montey is coming here? As in *the* Marco Montey? The race-car driver?"

"Yeah," Jennifer confirmed, crossing her arms in

front of her chest. "Apparently he graduated from the University of Texas and has family here. And if the tabloids have him nailed, he can't stand living an entire day without tempting fate." She slanted her gaze toward Ryan. "Thus, his new love affair with him."

"Can I meet Montey?" Sabrina asked both Jennifer and Ryan. "Or rather interview him?" Pushing past the ingrained need for privacy despite Ryan's presence, she turned an appeal on Jennifer, "I follow racing so I can hold my own with him. I won't embarrass you. And Montey is notorious for joking around with the press and telling them absolutely nothing about his life, or his future career plans. And right now, he's in a dispute with his sponsor, Can Cola, for drinking Red Rock Cola on camera. If I can get the scoop on that and more, this will be my opportunity to prove to Frank I can deliver compelling stories that have nothing to do with my father's politics. I know you know what that means to me. Please." She glanced between the two of them. "I really need this interview."

"I don't know," Jennifer said tentatively. "Ryan? Can she interview Montey? Can you get him to talk—as in really talk to her? Not brush her off."

Sabrina fixed on Ryan sitting next to her, unaware of just how close they were until her knees brushed his. Heat darted up her thighs and thrummed through her core. "I…ah…" She stepped back a bit. "Sorry."

Eyes twinkling with mischief, he teased, "Running away when you want something from me isn't the best strategy, you know."

"Ryan!" Jennifer chided. "Will you behave?"

"Behaving is overrated," he said, his attention never leaving Sabrina, his eyes hot with challenge. "I'll make you a deal. If I can score you an interview, you go out with me."

Her stomach fluttered. An interview with Montey and a date with this wild cowboy. Montey was a building block of the new life she wanted. But at Ryan's bidding? An image of herself, strapped to a bed, Ryan naked and teasing her, had her all but visibly shaking herself to clear her head. Where the heck had that come from, and why did it arouse her so intensely?

Desperately, Sabrina focused her mind on the goal of a career-solidifying interview. "Does this date include jumping out of a plane?"

"Oh, good grief, Sabrina, you can't be considering this," Jennifer said, setting the paperwork on the desk. "I'll let you two work this out. And I'll be up front when you do."

Neither of them acknowledged Jennifer, either before or after her departure.

"Only if you want it to," Ryan replied to Sabrina's question, as if Jennifer had never spoken. Then he leaned toward her. "And for the record, I prefer you associate our first date with pleasure, not fear." He eased back, the scent of him, spicy and male, lingering in her senses, as he said, "Do we have a deal?"

Making a deal with this man wasn't safe. It wasn't something she would normally do.

"A date in exchange for an interview," she agreed, her resolve forming. "Yes. All right. We have a deal."

She wanted this interview. She wanted Ryan. And for once in her life, she wasn't denying herself just so she could be safe. She was embracing the thrill, the danger…and, yes, the deal.

Satisfaction slid across Ryan's face. "I've got your paperwork and contact information," he said. "I'll be in touch." He pushed to his feet.

"What?" she asked, suddenly uncertain about what had just happened. "How? When do I get my interview?"

Ryan snatched up the paperwork with all of her contact information. "When I come to collect my date." And then he sauntered toward the door.

"Wait," she said, following him. "Or rather. Should I wait here? Now?"

He paused in the doorway. "No need." He waved her papers at her. "I know how to find you and I will." He winked. "And that, sweetheart, is a promise you can label absolute." He disappeared into the hallway. Sabrina swayed, her fists balled by her sides, as she fought the urge to go after him. Resisted the urge to try and control what she couldn't control. And she was pretty darn sure she could no more control Ryan Walker than she could repress that burn inside her to give it her best try.

4

SHE NEEDED THIS INTERVIEW with Marco to solidify her new life in Texas. And not just a standard interview like the one the Mayor gave at his press conference about supporting the troops, and how this soldier turned bank robber had a stress disorder brought on by combat, which so many ex-military have, as well. In this case, she wasn't sure that was the real story. Especially since she'd gotten home to an email from Frank, with a snapshot of the soldier and his family, a wife and two kids, who looked very happy together. The email had read "My contact says wife has visited the Mayor's office after hours and her name was erased from the visitation log."

It wasn't in her nature to not fight for people who needed help. The idea that the wife might need hers, well, it was getting to her a little. She'd dig around some but she wasn't telling Frank she was doing it. And in the meantime, she wanted that interview with Marco Montey—an interview she'd make into something that spoke to race-car lovers and managed to show off her talents as a journalist. Not sure how she would do that, but she'd figure it out.

Exactly why Sabrina's cell phone sat on the edge of her new, fancy marble tub. The tub had tempted her into renting a condo with an option to buy, but she wouldn't be able to afford it if she didn't get her career on track. Thus why, in the far-too-many hours that had passed since her "deal" with Ryan, she'd done plenty of that worrying she'd sworn was a good thing; the knots in her stomach begged to differ. Plain and simple, she was fretting herself sick that she'd soon be leaving her high ceilings and shiny wooden floors for a cramped New York apartment with only a shower once again. Because that was exactly what was going to happen if she were going to report on politics, as Frank would have it. She'd get paid a whole lot more for it in New York where she had a reputation. Remaining here wouldn't serve any purpose, no matter how tempted she was to stay the course.

And it seemed temptation had led her to all kinds of places lately. To this condo, and now straight into the path of Ryan, who she couldn't get out of her head. Or her bath, she realized guiltily. Every time she closed her eyes, she imagined him here, naked—water dripping off sleek muscles that she would lick dry. Grrrrr. There she went again!

Anxious to put an end to the unbearable waiting, Sabrina glanced at the lit-up face of her cell phone. Nine o'clock. The chances of good news at this late hour were slim, and she resisted the urge to be pushy and dial Jennifer. The truth was, the disappointment sprang from more than the interview. It was about Ryan and his "deal." About the excuse that deal gave her to go where she didn't belong with the man. It was Ryan who could give her Marco. Ryan who could give her…

"More than you can handle," she murmured, rising to her feet in a splash of bath water, and reaching for a fluffy white towel she'd bought at a Macy's summer blow-out sale at about half the price of a New York summer blow-out sale. She could get used to these prices for sure. Even her morning Starbucks was cheaper, which helped justify the price of her condo. She liked this city. Austin had an artsy, contemporary feel, the music and movie scene, without the hustle and bustle of Manhattan. Maybe she didn't have to go home to be home, and maybe she'd even be okay writing about the political scene here, with distance from her father. Her chest tightened. Or maybe not.

She knotted the towel firmly around her chest and padded across the thick teal-blue bathroom rug to the mirror above the stainless-steel sink, where she glanced at her hair piled atop her head in disarray. She looked like a wreck, felt like a wreck. Not one bit sexy, despite the sex on her mind.

She pursed her lips. "You aren't having sex with Ryan 'Cowboy' Walker, nor are you ever going to," she murmured in denial of her yearning for this man. With a regretful sigh, she opened the mahogany cabinet, snatching the new mud mask that the mall clerk had convinced her was the ticket to radiance.

"No sex with Ryan," she told her image in the mirror, "so stop thinking about it."

With determination to do just that, she spread the green goop all over her face. Task complete, she was satisfied that for the duration of her hour-long facial, she would not only look like Frankenstein, but all sexual urges would be diluted.

She'd only just traded her towel for her silver silk knee-length robe and started for the long hallway leading to the sunken living room, when a knock sounded on the door.

With a frown, she hesitated outside the red "good luck" door—as the real-estate agent had called it—certain that whoever was outside wasn't going to agree it was lucky if he or she saw her in this mask.

Still, what real choice did she have? She called out, "Who is it?"

"It's your jumpmaster, sweetheart," came the deep, familiar voice she knew as that of temptation himself. "Open up."

Sabrina's heart skipped a beat. A rush of adrenaline ran through her veins.

"You owe me a date," he said. "I came to collect."

"You owe me an interview," she called out. This couldn't be happening. Not with mud on her face. "You can't just show up here unannounced."

"Not even if I tell you Marco is in the car waiting for us to drive him to the airport?"

Marco was here? Without thinking, she flung the door open. "He's here? As in at my condo? You got me the interview?" She'd barely spat out the questions before she realized what she'd done. Big gorgeous Ryan loomed above her, his arm resting on the frame above his head, amusement in his eyes as he took in her silk robe and the mess on her face. She'd fantasized about losing control with Ryan, and now she had. In the most unsexy of ways.

She squeezed her eyes shut, but not before she noticed his hat was gone, his mussed sandy-brown hair neat to the naked eye. "I'm going to close the door now, and please pretend this never happened."

RYAN WASN'T ABOUT to forget one moment of Sabrina in a skimpy robe.

"Afraid I can't do that," Ryan answered, advancing on Sabrina with nothing short of a predatory stride. In a flash, he had maneuvered them through the doorway and inside the condo, the door kicked shut behind him. And because he was but a man, with only so much restraint, he tugged the silk of her robe over the swell of high, full breasts, barely concealed. "Not when you're teasing me with so much skin. Your robe was gaping."

She quickly reached for the opening, her hands colliding with his, her gaze lifting in a panicked flutter of dark lashes on pale skin. "I… This is so not going well."

"I'm not sure I agree," he said. "Though taking your clothes off would be a lot more enjoyable than putting them on. I won't ask about the green stuff on your face as long as it won't stop me from kissing you."

"You can't be serious," she said, her voice raspy, breathless. "It'll get it all over you. And what about Marco?"

"Marco knew he had to wait," he said. He could almost taste her. He wanted to taste her. To hell with the damn mask. "And I'm a soldier, sweetheart. I like getting dirty." His hand wrapped the back of her neck, drawing her closer, his lips lingering above hers. "And unless you tell me not to and fast, I'll demonstrate."

"Ryan—" The one word was a whisper, an invitation, a *yes* in his book. He took it, swallowed it, angling his lips over hers. She was sweet and delicious, and everything he'd imagined for the hours since meeting her… and so much more.

Her mouth was soft and alluring, her tongue tentatively responding to his demands. She tasted both exotic and sweet, bold and tentative. A woman who had so much to offer but was afraid to give or take. It was the fear in her that kept his hands from traveling her body, that told him to go slow, to give her time. That she would be worth it. But she moaned, the sound driving him wild, urging him to touch, to take. And her hands—caressing a reserved path up his chest and around his neck—they were the ingredient that nearly set him on edge, them and her touch—knowing that only a tiny piece of silk separated him from her, from the pale ivory skin he'd already admired. Everything male in him screamed to repair that fact, to rip away the robe, to fill his hands with her breasts. He imagined the moment in his mind, damn near tasted how sweet it would be. And then his cell phone rang a rude awakening.

"That'll be Marco," he murmured against her lips.

Sabrina groaned and backed away. "I have to get dressed. I have to get this mask off my face." Her eyes went wide, and she laughed, her finger running down his cheek. "At least I'm not the only one with mud on my face now. You—"

Ryan silenced her with his mouth. Damn, she was adorable. Gently, but no less forcefully, his hand went to her neck again, and he kissed her with a long, quick slide of his tongue. "We'll finish this later," he vowed, all too aware of how easily she would then talk herself out of "later." "You have about three minutes to get ready. Now go."

"I'll think about the 'later' thing," she replied with a stern facade she couldn't maintain. An instant later, a smile touched her lips. "I wasn't joking about the mud on your face. The spare bathroom is on the other side of the kitchen if you want to clean up." Her smile widened. "I'll be back in a flash."

Not fast enough, Ryan thought. He couldn't remember the last time a woman had him so hot and hard, so ready. She rushed down the hallway—all but running. Oh, yeah, she was running. He'd seen it in her eyes today at the Hotzone. He knew the look all too well, because he'd once done the same. He'd run and found the military. He wondered what Sabrina was running from. He understood she had issues to work through. She'd be emotional, distant, then wild when she finally let herself go. She'd need someone to use and abuse, without any demands beyond pleasure. Someone like him, who didn't mind a little mud on his face. His lips lifted. It was a tough job, but someone had to do it.

5

SABRINA COULDN'T BELIEVE she was sliding into the back of a Town Car to interview the hottest man on the tracks, with the sexiest cowboy in Texas right next to her. A sexy cowboy whom she'd just kissed. With a mud mask in place. Which had gotten all over him, and she didn't have the heart to tell him it was still smudged near his ear, though she had no idea how it had gotten there.

His ear wasn't exactly where her mouth had been, though it was a nice ear, worthy of attention. Everything about Ryan demanded attention. In fact, it was especially hard to remember why she had thought Ryan was more dangerous than jumping out of a plane, when the taste of him still lingered on her lips despite her clean-scrubbed face.

"You must be Sabrina," Marco said, turning the full magnitude of his blond, city-sleek good looks, high cheekbones and intelligent eyes on her. Yet, all she could think about was the thigh of her rough, tough cowboy settling beside hers. Marco cast her an amused glance, taking in her bare face and piled-high hair, as well as her black sweat suit, the only thing she could manage in the two minutes she'd had to get dressed. "I told Ryan to warn you I was coming."

"I've only just met Ryan, but I think it's safe to say he likes to shake things up." She cut him a reprimanding stare. "Namely me."

"And you like it," Ryan assured her with a wink, before tugging the door shut, darkness consuming them as the overhead light shut off. Ryan's thigh melted into hers, a shiver of awareness shimmied up her spine and back down.

Marco tapped the back of the driver's seat, sparing Sabrina a witty comeback her brain simply wasn't producing. "Drive like you were me," Marco ordered. "I have a plane to catch."

"If I could drive like you," the man behind the wheel said, "I wouldn't be shuttling you around. But I'll give it my best shot." The man hit the accelerator, and the car jerked into motion.

Sabrina jerked with it, her oversize purse with her notepad, pen and recorder tumbling to the floor at Ryan's feet. Instinctively, she reached for something solid to keep from falling. That something solid turned out to be Ryan's jeans-clad leg, the one she'd been admiring earlier. Instantly, his hand came down on hers, holding it captive. Her gaze snapped to his, and the twinkle of his eyes cut through the inky shadows.

"I assume Ryan warned you my sister is a big fan," Marco commented from her left.

"Big fan?" she echoed, the question barely permeating the lusty Ryan-formed clouds muddling her brain. "I'm sorry. What did I miss?" She glanced between the two men, all too aware that her hand remained trapped beneath Ryan's bigger, stronger one—on his thigh, impossible for Marco to miss.

"Sabrina and I didn't get much time to talk," Ryan replied, releasing her hand and settling into his seat.

"What didn't we talk about that we should have?" she asked, wondering why her hand still tingled where Ryan had held it.

"It seems today is all about deals," Ryan said, no mistaking his meaning. "Marco's sister was with him at the Hotzone when I brought up the interview," Ryan explained. "She knew you instantly from your column in the *New York Prime*."

"And the bargaining began," Marco said, with a disgusted snort. "She might as well be a politician. Oh, wait. She is. She's on the city council with aspirations of more."

Sabrina's stomach tightened. "Oh, really," she said, trying to fight the tension in her voice.

"Here's the situation, Sabrina. My sister's been trying to convince me to speak at some political fundraiser—and I won't mention for which party because I try not to talk preferences. It gets me in trouble with the press."

"Like drinking Red Rock Cola?" she asked, trying to

change the subject from anything that involved politics and where his sister was headed.

He laughed. "Exactly like drinking Red Rock Cola. That's what I get for being thirsty and drinking what someone pushed into my hand."

"Can I quote you on that?"

"Wait for the interview," he said.

"So this isn't the interview?" she asked, frustrated they were back to his sister, and a bargain for an interview with him. As in, Sabrina speaking at that political fundraiser in his place.

"Marco's not asking you to take his place or I wouldn't have brought him here, Sabrina," Ryan said, seemingly reading her mind. "You have my word."

His word—a loosely given vow uttered by many a politician. But Ryan wasn't a politician, she reminded herself. He was a darn good kisser, and the man who'd gotten her in the car with Marco Montey.

"All I promised Calista was a chance to talk to you," Marco assured her. "Speak or don't speak at that engagement of hers. It's of zero consequence to me. I did my part by arranging a call. In return, she stops pestering me about you, and you get your interview. As in a full, no-time-constraint interview—by phone, if you can deal with that. I'll talk to you like no one else I talk to, on one condition. No politics. I know that's your thing, but I don't talk politics. Like I said, it pisses off my sponsors. Hell, I don't even vote."

"You don't vote?" she asked before she could stop herself.

Marco pointed at her. "No politics, remember?"

Okay, fine. Good actually. She tested him to be sure. "I won't speak at your sister's political event."

Marco smiled. "Then don't," he said. "And yes, you still get your interview." He reached into his bag on the floor and pulled out a can of Can Cola and popped the top. "Be sure you mention I was drinking this when you met me." He wiggled his eyebrows. "Your interview request was well timed. I need some good press right now."

Relief washed over her. This interview was going to happen and she had Ryan to thank for it. Ryan whom she had kissed. Ryan who was daring and dangerous. Ryan who made her hot, and considering they were in the same car—was most likely going back to her apartment with her.

A FEW MINUTES LATER, the short ride to the airport was over, the call to Calista and the interview with Marco had been arranged.

"The driver will take you back to your place," Marco told her with a smile. "Talk to you soon." Marco exited the car, leaving her and Ryan alone. Sitting next to each other. Close. Her mind raced—okay, stumbled—over what to do next. Move? Don't move? Why wasn't she moving? Wouldn't moving be running? She couldn't run. This was supposed to be the life she took charge of. This was the life in which she dictated what came next.

Ryan's cell rang, and Sabrina said a silent thank-you

for the reprieve. She slid to the other side of the car to give him space to snatch his phone off his belt and glance at the ID. She wasn't running. She was simply being...courteous.

Ryan silenced the ringer and ignored the caller, then snatched her purse and held it out to her about the time the muffled ring of her cell radiated through the black leather.

"That'll be Jennifer," he said, as she accepted her purse. "I'm sure she wants to know how the meeting went with Marco." He settled his back against his door again. "And if I managed to keep my hands off you as ordered."

That was a conversation she wasn't about to have in front of Ryan. And he knew it. She set her purse down. "I guess I'll call her and let her know about Marco. And we both know you already failed the hands-off promise."

"I didn't promise," he said. "She talked. I listened. Guess she's afraid I'll offend the delicate sensibilities of the politician's daughter."

"I do not have delicate sensibilities." Sabrina bristled, folding her arms across her chest.

He arched a brow. "Jennifer appears to think you do."

"Maybe she simply thinks you're trouble," she said.

"Then maybe you should run," he suggested.

Run. That darn word again. "I don't run."

"Then why'd you leave New York?"

Now he was making her mad. "Why'd you leave the Army?"

He stared at her and chuckled. "I had my reasons."

"And so did I."

His lips twitched. "Copy that. Then I guess we understand each other."

Understand each other? "I doubt that."

"No?" he asked.

"Highly improbable."

"Because of your delicate sensibilities," he teased.

She leaned forward and pointed. "Don't push me," she chided.

He leaned forward, close. "Can't help myself." His eyes twinkled with mischief. Sexy, wonderful mischief that made her feel more alive and turned-on than she had in a very long time.

A few seconds ticked by. Gray and white shadows swirled with passing reflections. It occurred to her she wanted to kiss him. Her. Kiss. Him. Not the other way around. If they held their positions much longer, he'd kiss her and then she'd never know if she had the courage to go first.

She leaned back and crossed her arms again. He mimicked her position, arms in front of his broad, gorgeous chest. Silence ensued as did an outright stare-off. Sexual tension inked a path from him to her. Or maybe it was her to him because everything about the man, from his demanding personality to the scar she had just located right above his top lip—that really full, sexy lip—did a number on her. Proven by the damp tingling feeling in the V of her body. A sensation she found downright unnerving, considering the man was several arm lengths away.

She wanted to forget everything with Ryan and just experience him. To let go. But how could she after the political attachment that had come with Marco, through him? Ryan, who had kissed her. Ryan, who she wanted to kiss her again. Ryan, who she'd considered dangerous because he excited her, scared her, made her want to toe some invisible line that felt erotic and daring.

Yet, she'd never considered he could have a political agenda, or that he might sell her out to someone who did. He seemed too true-blue for that. Still…

"Do you vote, Ryan?"

"Call me paranoid," he said, "but it seemed a bad idea to vote for, or against, anyone who might later be assigning me a death mission."

The last thing she'd call Ryan was paranoid. Or safe. Was he teasing her again? "Soldiers get secret ballots like the rest of us."

"I wasn't just a soldier," he said. "In fact, for all practical purposes, I didn't exist. If I went on a mission and didn't come back, I just didn't come back."

"Are you saying you were afraid to vote?"

"Careful now," he warned in a teasing voice. "Us tough-guy soldiers take issue with being called afraid. Besides, most of the time, I was so deep inside enemy territory, I couldn't be found if you wanted to hand me a ballot. Only a few people knew of my missions."

"A person can't just disappear," she said softly. "Your family would miss you. They'd ask questions."

His lashes lowered to half-veil, a split second of heavy silence falling before he replied, "The Army *was* my family."

Translation. He was alone. As in, no parents to drive him crazy, but still love him insanely, as hers did. No matter how she tried to escape her family's craziness, the insane-love part was never in doubt and always comforting.

A million questions flew through her mind, but she settled for, "Yet, you left."

"Like I said," he replied, "I had my reasons."

Suddenly, he moved, and he was leaning over her, his arms framing either side of her shoulders. "Ask me the question that's on your mind. The real one. Not something you say because you're on the spot."

She inhaled a sharp breath, laced with the spicy, warm scent of him, his mouth close. His kiss a promise she wanted to make reality. And she didn't play coy. She hated coy. She liked straightforward. She liked direct. She liked what you see is what you get. And she needed to know if that was what Ryan was going to give her. So she asked the question he wanted to hear, the question she most wanted answered. "What do you want from me, Ryan?"

"You," he said. "Just you."

The claim, spoken in his deep baritone voice, delivered raw sensuality. A shiver raced down her spine, and it was all she could do not to pull his mouth to hers but…the driver. She squeezed her eyes shut as she accepted the part of her life that relocating could not change. She hated that she cared about gossip, hated that even with a man like Ryan so close she could taste him, she remembered how easily a third party could spread rumors, how easily those rumors could become poison to a political career like her father's. Sabrina ached to feel free.

"Sabrina, look at me," Ryan ordered, his tone rough with a low command, his breath warm on her lips.

She leaned forward and pressed her mouth to his.

Instantly, his hands framed her face, his mouth slanting over hers, his tongue gently parting her lips. He tasted her deeply, sensually, drawing her into the moment. Coaxing her to forget everything but the way his tongue drew on hers. The way his body felt beneath her palms that had somehow come to rest on his broad shoulders. Another caress of his lips, another slide of his tongue. Her hands slid around his neck.

His hand rested on her hipbones, long fingers wrapping around her waist, fingers that slid intimately over her ribs. Brushed the curve of her breast. Her nipples tightened, she clenched her thighs, suddenly realizing Ryan was between them. Crazy panic overcame her. A picture, a tabloid story. She had to get up. She… Ryan kissed her long and hard, driving away the thoughts before announcing, "We're here."

She glanced around to realize they had, indeed,

arrived at her condo, and, with their arrival, she had escaped the dilemma of the driver, and found another. The moment of truth. There were no barriers, no cameras, no hiding inside her apartment. Not with Ryan there with her.

6

RYAN HELPED SABRINA out of the Town Car and barely contained a chuckle as she darted away. He'd never known a woman so conflicted in so many ways. And difficult. And sexy. He couldn't wait to unravel the secrets beneath the prim and proper politician's daughter. And the idea that he'd be the only man to know those secrets well…

"If I'm not back in thirty minutes, leave without me," Ryan ordered the driver before slamming the door shut.

He turned to find Sabrina gaping at him. She opened her mouth and then snapped it shut, before turning on her heels and marching toward her building. Ryan's pursuit was instant, and while he could have caught up to her before she entered the building, he waited until she was striding across the fancy black-and-white marble floor toward the elevator inside. Then, and only then, did he grab her hand and pull her around to face him.

"Do you not understand discretion, Ryan?" she huffed

out instantly, her cute, pointed chin tilted up, green eyes flashing with warning. Voice urgent but hushed. "My father plans to run for President. If that driver tells the tabloids I'm off in Texas, whoring around, he'll never get there."

Ryan scrubbed a hand over his face. President. Okay. He didn't see that one coming. "The driver doesn't know who you are. We never mentioned a name, just an address."

"Maybe he knows who I am and maybe he doesn't," she said. "But I don't have the luxury of taking that risk. My private life has to be my private life. That I can't change by moving. I wish I could but I can't. The minute a politician runs for higher office, people crawl out of the woodwork to tell their stories, truth or fiction. I don't want to be one of those stories."

He stopped, checked himself. He didn't want to leave and that was where this was headed. He wanted this woman next to him, beneath him, wanted her calling his name. He vowed to do whatever it would take. It didn't matter that she was finding herself and would, no doubt, carry her fine little backside right back to New York. There was here. There was now. And there was a father running for President.

Another silent curse followed, as he reined in his control, and gained a new respect for Sabrina in the process. He'd chosen to be a soldier and chosen when not to be. She was hungry to have choices and still felt without them.

"I'll leave." But he didn't let go of her hand; he

couldn't make himself. Instead his fingers gently stroked her palm.

A conflicted look flashed across her face, torment showed in her gorgeous green eyes before her dark lashes swept low on ivory cheeks, lingered and then lifted.

"Right," she said softly. "You'd better."

Disappointment, regret, laced the words. And she didn't move any more than he did. Didn't make any effort to distance herself from him. She swallowed, her delicate neck moving with the action, her hand—tiny and delicate—still in his.

Ryan studied her, searching for answers with the same intent he would the members in a mission. Analyzing the emotions he saw in her. Understanding. She didn't want him to go. She didn't want him to let her go so easily. She wanted an escape. And now, she expected him to turn around and walk out the door. Well, Ryan had never been one to do the expected. He wasn't going to start with Sabrina. Not with his blood pumping liquid fire.

He tightened his hand on hers and led her toward the stairwell.

"What are you doing?" Sabrina whispered behind him. "Ryan!"

He didn't reply. She'd find out his intention soon enough. There was something about Sabrina he likened to the adrenaline rush he got the minute the plane door opened and he knew the world was about to explode around him in some mad, uncertain, amazing way. Just once in her life, Sabrina needed to feel that feeling. And he was going to be the man to show her how.

Ryan yanked open the stairwell door, scanned for cameras and found none. Tugged Sabrina forward and pressed her back against the closed door, framing her legs with his. Nuzzled the thickness of his erection against her stomach. He could smell her, damn near taste her. Oh yeah, he was gonna taste her all right. In all kinds of ways.

Her hands went to his chest. "Ryan! Are you crazy?!" Her green eyes glistened with flecks of amber warmth. It wasn't normally a woman's eyes he got lost in, but then, he was normally restricted to a dark bar and a quick goodbye before another mission. This time, the woman was his mission.

"Daring," he corrected, wrapping a hand around her neck to bring her to him. "Like you want to be."

"What are you doing?" she demanded, raspy, aroused, sexy as hell.

"Someone will see us! What about cam—"

He kissed her—no, he drank her as he had the cool, perfect water that had saved his life not so long ago, in a place he'd rather forget. This kiss, this woman—neither one did he want to forget, nor did he expect he ever would.

"NO CAMERAS."

Sabrina had barely processed Ryan's statement before his lips once again possessed hers in another drugging, impossible-to-resist kiss, sweeping her into a deep, lust-filled haze. She struggled for sanity, willed her hands to shove Ryan away, instead losing herself in the rich, male taste of him. Desperately, she struggled to remain stiff and unyielding, failing miserably. Every slow, sensual stroke of Ryan's tongue against hers drew her deeper into a spell, and slowly, slowly, her fingers softened against his hard muscle rather than trying to press him away from her.

A tiny part of her brain continued to scream with the fear of being caught, with the frustration of having to worry at all. But Ryan's touch, his tongue, his taste—it was all too much to resist. With a moan, she arched into his touch, his hands sliding across her back, caressing her into a burning need she wasn't sure she could fight, wasn't sure she wanted to fight.

This was what people talked about when they said they were consumed with need. She knew now. Had never understood before.

Another caress of his hand, another caress of his tongue, another rush of his spicy male scent, and worry slid away, the stairwell with it. Ryan was everything, Ryan was her next breath.

Abandonment came with a rush of passion and Sabrina suddenly couldn't get close enough to him. She pressed to her toes, reaching urgently for more of his mouth. Moaned when he deepened the kiss, a plea for more in the wordless demand. She reached for his shirt and worked her hand under the cotton, desperate to touch him. Sighing with the warmth of his skin, warm all over, she was just plain hot.

He cupped her breasts, thumbing her nipples through her T-shirt. Her mind conjured an image of his mouth on her nipple. His lips found her jaw, her neck, and her head fell back against the door, welcoming the erotic invasion. Frustration rolled inside her as a tiny sliver of familiar fear and guilt slid into her consciousness and threatened to steal this escape. "I shouldn't be doing this," she whispered roughly, unconvincing even to her own ears.

"I told you," he said, his hand sliding under her shirt and over her breast again, teeth nipping her earlobe. "No worrying." He shoved down her bra and tweaked her nipple.

A gasp fell from her lips, his name with it. "Ryan."

He kissed his name from her lips. "Sabrina," he murmured, his tongue caressing hers, his hips shifting, lowering, his thick erection pressing against her, promising satisfaction. "Trust me."

Cynically, she laughed. "The famous words uttered at just the right moment from someone who wants something."

"But you really can trust me," he assured her, dropping to one knee, his hands on her hips, her waist, inching up her shirt. His breath was warm on the V of her body. Shock rushed over her, mingled with uncontrollable arousal.

"What are you doing?" she demanded urgently. "Get up. Someone is going to find us."

"No one will find us," he promised, his lips touching her bare stomach, his tongue dipping into her belly button. "Relax." His fingers worked the side of her pants down as his lips grazed her hips.

"Ohh," she murmured, swallowing hard. "Stop. We have to..." He tugged her sweats farther down and slid a hand over her bare backside.

"No panties," he said approvingly, his fingers curving her backside, brushing the crevice of her cheek and taking her pants farther down. His mouth explored her stomach, her hips. Every nip and lick quivered through her body. Wetness clung to her thighs, aching need spiraled inside her. Her fingers slid to his head as she silently willed his mouth where she wanted it. His mouth moved lower, closer to where she wanted him, but a second of clarity sparked renewed panic.

Sabrina's fingertips dug into his shoulders. "Wait! No! We are going to get caught, Ryan. I can't. We can't."

He glanced up at her, one long finger sliding along the slick sensitive flesh between her thighs, his eyes dark and sultry, wickedly intent.

Her breath lodged in her throat, her flashes fluttered. "Oh, Ryan."

Two fingers slid inside her, drawing out her gasp, and then uncontrollably, the arch of her hips. "That's it, sweetheart," he said. "Forget the door. We've blocked this one, and we'll hear the one above if it opens." His fingers explored, pumped. Sabrina bit her lip, then panted, unable to stop herself from rocking against his hand. "So wet," he said. "So sexy." His mouth came down on her stomach again. She was panting, her nipples aching, and she barely stopped herself from touching them. She'd never done anything as daring as this. She shouldn't be doing this. But it felt so good, he felt so good. And… Oh, his mouth closed down on her, suckling the swollen bud of her clit.

"Ryan. Ohh. I can't…I…please, Ryan…" *Don't stop. Don't stop licking and suckling and…touching.*

Every objection faded to pants and moans she barely recognized as her own. All time slipped away. All concept of fear, danger. There was only the bliss of those fingers, those lips, his tongue. And yes, the danger. It was exciting, intense. Taking her for a ride, a wild, wicked ride, until she was tumbled into release with a jerk of her hips. All but shaking, little darts of tension fluttering low in her stomach, rippling through her and tightening into a ball of fire deep in her core. His fingers worked against her, caressed against the spasms tightening around them. Then slowed, as the spasms slowed. Easing her to a final ripple and then to awareness. Her hand covered her face, her hair was in her eyes but she didn't care. What had she done? What had he done to her? What did she do now? Suddenly, Ryan kissed her stomach, and, with skill no man should possess—or maybe every man should possess—he righted her clothes with the same, quick ease with which he'd undressed her. She let him, too. She couldn't seem to make herself move, unsure of herself. What did one say after an orgasm in a stairwell? Thanks? How about a bed next time? Or even a couch? Goodnight? Yes. She needed to say goodnight. To regroup. To… He finished restoring her clothes and Sabrina darted forward in escape. Or she tried.

"Oh, no, you don't," Ryan said softly, and suddenly, she was wrapped in his arms, his lips close, and those long, sturdy thighs of his molded to her own. "I'm not done with you yet."

7

SABRINA COULDN'T BELIEVE Ryan's lips were on hers again. She should be mad at his rather assuming words, *I'm not done with you yet.* She would be had any other man said that. But that deliciously firm mouth of his swept across her lips, not once but twice, stealing her objections before the slightest hint of tongue brushed hers.

He paused, only a breath from her mouth, as if he couldn't make himself pull away. And that funny, unidentifiable flutter in her chest that Sabrina had felt once before expanded and stretched again. She'd been right to call him dangerous. This man made her forget everything but him—logic, reason, stairwells where she should not be getting naked. She had no idea what he was doing to her, but she knew she liked it too much.

Slowly, Ryan pulled back, fixing her in a warm inspection. "As much as I'd loved to walk you to your door and convince you to let me make it happen again, I have a ride to catch." One corner of his gorgeous mouth lifted. "Discretion and all, you know."

"It's a little late for discretion," she objected, a warm flush climbing up her neck at the image in her mind of her leg over his shoulder, her pants gone, while he did intimate, amazing, out-of-line and improper things to her. And to her dismay, she could feel the warm, wet heat regathering in the V of her body. And that made her mad. At herself. At him for having so much control over her. How had she let this situation get so out of control? "What if someone saw us?"

His hands slid to her face. "No one knows but you and me." His voice lowered slightly, took on a promise. "And they never will." He released her and sidestepped to grab the door and glanced back. "You still owe me a date."

And then to her utter disbelief, he left. Ryan had just given her an orgasm in the stairwell of her building and left. Wait! This couldn't happen. She couldn't leave things like this. She couldn't. Had she just used him? Or had he used her?

Seemed Ryan had a way of making her act without thinking, because she charged forward and after him. She needed something more than...well, an orgasm. Which was ironic because with most of the guys in her life, she'd have killed for just that.

Sabrina yanked the door open just in time to see the lobby door shut. She pursued, her heart racing as fast as her feet could take her. She exited to the warm Texas night right as the car pulled away.

SABRINA SIGHED AND RESTED her elbow on the coffee table. She sat on the floor in front of the couch, her Austin City skyline view streaked with yellows and reds as the sun sprayed the sky with morning flavor.

Sunday morning had arrived far too slowly considering sleep had been nowhere to be found. By 6:00 a.m. Sabrina had been up and making a pot of coffee. And now, at seven, she was fully dressed in her favorite faded jeans and a cool Harley Davidson shirt she'd picked up a few blocks away. Totally inappropriate for her father's daughter, whom her mother had insisted be prim and proper at every public outing. But that only made her love the shirt more.

She had secret fantasies about riding a Harley and about riding a man who rode a Harley. A man like Ryan, she thought. She laughed to herself, thinking how appalled her mother would be. She loved her mother, but sometimes Sabrina thought her mother would benefit from a Harley fantasy or two of her own. When was the last time she'd seen her mother smile—really smile—not plaster on a camera-ready mockery of one?

Sipping from her mug, Sabrina savored the caffeine, and then punched a key or two on her notebook computer, trying to bring into focus an idea she had brewing for a six-part feature on race-car driving, highlighting everything from drivers to mechanics. But all she saw was Ryan. Ryan, who'd undressed her in the stairwell. Ryan, who'd left her in that stairwell. Ryan, who'd lured her to an indiscretion, yet had still somehow, in the end, given her discretion.

"Stop it, Sabrina," she murmured. Stop thinking about Ryan. Frustrated with herself, Sabrina splayed fingers into her freshly washed hair and then she did exactly what she'd told herself not to do. Thought of Ryan. Of his claim that she still owed him a date. Right. Of course. He probably thought she was all kinds of easy. Why wouldn't he want to go out with her? She'd be a fast track to bedroom bliss. Or… maybe he wouldn't call at all. Maybe he would lose interest, considering how easy she'd been. Then she could worry for the rest of her life that Ryan would suddenly be one of those people who came out of the woodwork and told the world she was a hussy right when her father needed her to be an angel. For that kind of worry, she should at least have held out for the whole package—naked man and a long, hot night. But no. She'd settled for a stairwell. She deserved what she was feeling.

She groaned and forced herself to focus on her computer. But instead of looking up Marco and working on the interview that needed to be perfect to stake her claim on a new writing genre, she searched the press-conference topic—the soldier turned-bank-robber-and-drug-dealer. She opened her email and found the name of the contact in the mayor's office that Frank had given her, and made the call.

Thirty minutes later, she hung up, with not much more info than what she already had. A secretary in the Mayor's office had been working late, and swore she saw the wife of the dead soldier there. Nothing more than what Frank had told her, and not enough to say the meeting took place. The secretary could be mistaken, or looking for her fifteen minutes of fame. Sabrina knew the wife was MIA, number disconnected, house vacant, no forwarding address, since she'd suggested Frank send a reporter to her house. She emailed Frank to see if he'd had any luck locating the wife. She was sure she'd regret it because he would see this as her admission that she wanted this story. And she didn't, not really. Maybe, but someone else could take the credit, then, at least, she'd know the story that needed to be told was told. If even there was a story, she reminded herself.

With a grimace, Sabrina pushed to her feet and headed toward the kitchen, carrying the Texas Longhorn mug she'd bought the same day she'd bought her T-shirt.

A knock sounded on the door. Her heart fluttered hopefully, and she immediately shook her head in disgust. "You are out of control in so many ways," she muttered and set her coffee cup down. This time it really was going to be the kid next door, and she was actually hoping it was Ryan.

She didn't even allow herself a pause at the door. She yanked it open and then about swallowed her tongue. "Ryan," she choked out. All six foot and more of pure hot cowboy, minus the hat, his light-brown hair framing features as hard and strong as his body. And though his faded jeans, dusty boots and navy T-shirt might be simple, there was nothing simple about this man. Or about the way she reacted to him. He was everything she told herself she didn't need in a man, and everything the woman in her wanted.

"I brought breakfast," he said, sniffing the air. "Good. You've got the coffee." And just like that, he was inside, walking right past her and heading to the left, toward the kitchen.

"Ryan!" she challenged in disbelief. Good gosh, this man knew how to steal her equilibrium. She stepped into pursuit. "You can't just saunter in here uninvited. And do you realize it's seven in the morning?"

"Almost eight," he tossed over his shoulder. He paused briefly in the living room, eyed her window and whistled. "Nice view. I might have to get me one of those."

She caught up with him as he headed to the kitchen, forcing her to once again pursue. He set the bag of tasty treats on the wide, green-and-black granite counter that divided the kitchen from the rest of the open room. He grabbed a cup from a cabinet as if he knew exactly where to look and made the offhand remark, "Never knew I sauntered."

She pursed her lips and crossed her arms, trying not to notice the way his shirt tugged across hard muscle. "Like you own the place," she confirmed. "What if I'd been sleeping?"

He filled his cup—or her cup, that he'd now made his own, like her house. And her body. He seemed to take what he wanted, and it should irritate her.

"I figured you reporter types to be early risers," he commented matter-of-factly. "Us military types are the same way." He added several spoonfuls of sugar to his mug. Her gaze brushed the light-brown stubble on his jaw, now thicker, rougher. Very un-Army-like. Very… Harley rough—and tough. Dangerous and sexy. An image of him wearing a leather jacket and sitting on a Harley flashed in her mind.

"You a fan?"

Sabrina blinked at the question. Fan? What had she said and didn't remember saying? Or what was he saying? He seemed to read her blank stare and lifted his mug, mock-salute style. "Of the Longhorns," he offered.

"Ohhh," she said with relief—she had not spoken some part of her fantasy out loud, thankfully. "No. I mean, I figure I'm supposed to love the Longhorns to live here. The entire population wears orange like it's a second skin. You?"

"I'm from Houston," he said casually. "We aren't ravished by the UT football fever down there. Bobby has season passes, though. He assures me he'll make a follower out of me." His eyes twinkled, voice lowered slightly. "I'm finding Austin has plenty of appeal outside its college football."

Sabrina felt the heat in her cheeks, and was flustered by how easily Ryan drew a reaction. "You're an incorrigible flirt." She snatched the bag sitting on the counter. "And I deserve whatever is in this bag for putting up with it." She whirled on her heels with her best ice-princess persona—well practiced over the years as she mingled with newbie politicians who had tried to become her father, through her father. And through her.

A low, masculine rumble of laughter followed her, the sound dancing along her nerve endings and setting off a tingling along her spine. Sabrina sat down on the edge of the sofa cushion, spine stiff. It was Ryan's turn to pursue, and pursue he did, coffee mug in hand, carrying an air of ownership of everything around him.

She grimaced. "There you go again," she accused, because going on the attack was easier than melting like that pushover she feared he already thought her. "Sauntering over here like you own the place. You don't, you know."

"Man, woman," Ryan said, sitting down on the opposite end of the couch, leaving one cushion separating them. "I brought food. Be nice to me."

She tipped her chin up and opened the bag. "No."

"No?" he asked.

"You heard me," she said. "No."

Mischief gleamed in his eyes. "Why *no?*"

"Because you put me on the spot with Marco's sister," she said quickly. She couldn't shake how much it bothered her that Ryan had become entwined with politics. "And don't tell me Marco is giving me the interview no matter what. The pressure is there for me to say yes. You have no idea how tired I am of that kind of pressure, Ryan. You could at least have warned me in advance."

He gave her a thoughtful look. "You're right," he said, surprising her. "In all fairness, though, you distracted me by opening the door in that sexy-as-hell green muck of yours. I had to kiss you." She opened her mouth to object, and he quickly added, "I'm teasing. You're right. I should have warned you. I had no idea it would be as big a deal to you as it obviously is." He softened his tone, casting her a puppy-dog brown stare. "I'm sorry."

Oh, man, those eyes. He was good. Too good. "I'm not letting you off that easily."

"Why doesn't that surprise me?" he said, his eyes alight with amusement. "What do I have to do to make that up to you?"

Give me another orgasm, came her instant silent response, which was so out of character, it shook her into seeking a distraction. "I'll think about it while I eat," she replied. And curling her bare feet into the couch cushions, she took a bite of a yummy chocolate muffin. Deliciousness exploded in her mouth. "Oh, wow. This is so good."

"From the bakery on the corner," Ryan informed her, reaching into the bag for one of his own. "The clerk swore people come from all over town to get them so I figured we'd give 'em a go."

He took a bite of one of his own and quickly nodded his agreement with her assessment. "Not bad. Not bad at all." His gaze caught on the newspaper lying on the table, the cover story hers, though no one would know.

After penning the story, Sabrina hadn't been able to let the credit go to someone else, and she suspected Frank had known that would be the case. They'd settled on yet another pen name to keep her anonymous from the staff, which had allowed her to write from the heart. The governor had blamed post-traumatic stress disorder for the soldier's criminal activity, and after some research, Sabrina had found it wasn't uncommon for soldiers in wartime to suffer such problems and not be properly diagnosed and treated.

Ryan frowned and finished off his muffin. "That soldier didn't have post-traumatic stress disorder."

"How can you be so sure?" she asked, perking up with interest.

"I know," Ryan said.

Excitement started to form. "Are you saying you served with this man, Ryan? You knew him?"

"No," he said, quickly leaning forward to point out the newspaper.

There was a photo of the soldier, right before a sharpshooter killed him.

"See his wrist, right above the cuff? The symbol tattooed on his arm." Sabrina nodded and he showed her his own wrist. "That soldier was Special Ops. Unbreakable. He wasn't a trauma case. Ask yourself what was the bigger picture here."

There was an innuendo to those words that said he understood the soldier a bit more than he wished he did, and it made her curious. Why had he gotten out when he seemed so dedicated to being a soldier?

He slapped his legs. "Listen, your coffee has to be cold and my cup is empty." He headed to the kitchen, both their cups in hand. Surprised, Sabrina followed his path with her hungry stare. He was so, well, manly.

A soldier, honorable. A gentleman, filling her cup, not because it was expected, but because it was second nature. She could see that in his casual demeanor, his comfort in his own skin. Ryan seemed to just be Ryan. What you see is what you get, though the missions he'd run, the things he'd seen, said that might not be true. He confused her, he interested her. Too much. For the first time in a long time, she realized she might be able to fall for a guy. And get hurt. It was a frightening feeling. She had to rein this back in, get a grip, get some control. Starting now.

"How do you take your coffee?" he asked, rounding the end of the counter.

"Oh," she said, hopping to her feet in delayed reaction and rushing to the kitchen. "I was thinking I should have come to make it myself." In her haste, she'd put herself in her rather compact kitchen, with only inches separating her and Ryan.

They simply stood there, staring at each other, sexual tension snaking between them, sensuous in demand. Ryan took a step forward, and she stepped back. "Wait. Ryan. About last night." Okay. That wasn't exactly what she'd planned. "It was..."

He arched a brow. "It was...?"

Exciting. Scary. Perfect. Wrong. "A mistake."

One she would remember for the rest of her life.

8

"WHAT HAPPENED LAST NIGHT..." Ryan began, backing Sabrina against the counter and framing her legs with his own, the soft clean scent of her firing up his senses, "was hot. You were hot. We were hot. Everything about it was hot."

Her hands went to his shoulders, rejection in her soft features. "We almost had sex in the stairwell and that, by the way, is probably illegal."

"Did I mention it was hot?" he asked.

She blasted him with a look meant to ice the fire burning between them. It only stoked him further. Everything about her lit him up. "You're very sexy when you're mad."

Disbelief flickered in her face. "Are you trying to make me feel better or worse?" she demanded, and then cut her gaze, shoving at his chest. "Let me by. I can't do this, Ryan. That's not who I am."

Ryan held his steely position, gently capturing her wrists. "You think this is all about sex?"

Her eyes flashed with challenge, her cute pointed chin tilting upward. "Isn't it?"

"No," he said. "Or yes. I have no idea. How can I? How can you? We just met. But whether it turns out we're both living out some fantasy about a politician's daughter and a cowboy, or maybe something deeper, the only mistake is calling this a mistake before we find out."

Her lips parted. "A fantasy about a politician's daughter and a cowboy?"

"I'm teasing you," he said, running his hands up and down her slender waist. "Well, mostly teasing. Sabrina. Seriously. You just left New York. I just left the military. Let's explore together and see where it goes. Whatever you want, whatever you need, I'm the guy you can do it with, and it stays with me. Hell, I know government secrets that could get me killed."

"Killed?" she asked. "Who would kill you?"

He shook his head. "My point is that anything you want to explore with me is just with me. Between us. And if that is sex, or if it's a movie, or a place you want to go, or whatever, that's cool. Let's just have some fun and see where it goes. You're safe with me. In fact—" he released her and stepped back "—we won't have sex until you say we have sex. I won't pressure you. I won't even make a move. I'll want to and it'll be torture, but—" he held his hands up "—I'll wait until you say you're ready. Which, by the way, won't be easy, but I'm committed to the cause."

"I decide?" she asked, incredulously. "I can't decide."

"Why not?"

"That's too much pressure."

He wiggled an eyebrow. "We could spend the day making love and put the anticipation and nerves behind us. Certainly won't hear any complaints from me." Especially after he'd spent the entire night thinking about just that, something no other woman had ever done to him.

With a look of amazement, she accused, "You really say whatever comes to mind, don't you?"

He pressed his hands on the counter behind him. "Would you rather I play political word games?"

"No," she said quickly. "No political games, please. Most definitely not." Her hands went to her sides for emphasis. "Stay as you are."

Her answer pleased him, though he doubted she knew how poisonous those political games she'd come to despise could really be, or the blood they could spill. He did, though. He did and he'd left it behind.

"Then we agree," he said approvingly. "We shoot straight with each other. That leaves only having one last thing to address."

"Do I dare ask?" she teased, obviously relaxing a bit now. She laughed, a soft musical sound he felt like a punch in the gut. His groin tightened, zipper expanded. What the hell was he thinking, promising to keep his hands off her?

"You should always dare, darlin'," he told her, hoping she'd dare sometime soon. He snagged his wallet from his pocket, retrieving a business card. "We have to secure that interview of yours so I can secure my official date night." He was already punching a number into his cell.

"I'm supposed to call Calista Monday," she said and frowned. "Who are you calling?"

"Hey, Calista," Ryan said, noting with amusement the surprised, appalled look on Sabrina's face. "I have Sabrina here with me." He pressed his hand over the receiver and eyed Sabrina. "Can you talk to her now?"

"I can't believe you did this!" she whispered sharply. "I'm not prepared."

"Saying no doesn't require preparation," he said, and offered her the phone.

She pursed her lips and took the phone, covering the receiver. "I'm going to get you for putting me on the spot."

"Sounds fun," he teased.

Glowering, she promptly gave him her back, and then spoke into the phone. "Hi, yes. Thank you. I'm glad you enjoyed it. Yes. I... What time? Okay. Yes. I can find it. Sure. See you then."

She whirled on Ryan. "I have to go meet her for brunch at the Barton Creek Country Club."

"No, you don't," he said. "The deal was you talk to her, and you get your interview. You just talked to her."

"Talking to her means hearing her out, Ryan," she said. "I have to go."

"You don't."

"I do."

"I'll call Marco."

"No," she said, setting his phone on the granite counter. "I don't want to mess up in case he won't give me my interview. I need to go change. I have to meet her in an hour."

"No," he said, snagging her fingers in his before she got away. "You aren't changing for Calista. And there is no *if.* You don't want to do this, then don't do it."

"It's a pretty ritzy country club. I have to change. It's part of the requirements for a place like that."

"Screw the requirements," he said. "We'll pop by the country club. You tell her no to whatever it is she maybe wants you to do. Then I'll call Marco and confirm your interview."

"You don't have to go with me," she said, crossing her arms in front of her. "I can take care of myself."

He tugged her into his arms. "Of that, I have no doubt. But I got you into this. I owe it to you to make sure you get out of it. And call me self-serving, but I don't want you in the spotlight either. You'll never let yourself have any fun then." He grabbed the cell phone on the counter and eyed the time. "But you might have to help me look at a couple of houses. I stood the real-estate agent up yesterday. I don't want to do it again today. He says there are a couple of foreclosures that will go fast."

"You're buying a house?" she said, hands on her slender hips, where he'd like to put his.

He laughed. "That's right, I'm never going to convince Bobby and Caleb I'm here to stay if I don't put down some roots." He motioned with his chin. "What about you? This is a great place. Did you buy it?"

"Renting with the option to buy," she said, shoving her hands in her back pockets and looking a bit uncomfortable. "I need to be sure I can carve out a readership for my new pen name minus the political connections." She leaned a hip on the counter. "If I end up penning the same political stories I did back home, then ultimately that will expose my identity, and this has all been for naught."

"And you think Marco can help you carve out that readership?"

"I have an idea I think could really be great," she said. "Different. Something that will make me stand out."

"Tell me about this idea you have for Marco's interview on the drive to the country club," he suggested.

Ryan had a feeling no matter how much she stood out, she wouldn't be staying. Her father was headed for a run to the White House, and she'd go with him. This visit to Texas was a last chance to find herself before the microscope of her father's career honed in on her life. And Ryan was all about helping her do a little self-discovery and then letting her go. He was, after all, a master of short-term relationships, his life having allowed for nothing more. He'd honed the skill of saying goodbye with one foster family after another, and then one mission, one woman, one undercover identity at a time. This time would be no different…no matter how many nights Sabrina kept him awake dreaming about her.

RYAN MADE HER reach beyond her comfort zone, and that both scared and excited her. Walking into a ritzy country club in jeans and a Harley T-shirt, with a Harley-worthy man on her arm, was definitely outside of her comfort zone. It was something she never would have done back in New York. But entering the elegant restaurant inside the club, where elaborate flower arrangements hung from ceiling rafters and orchestra music drifted through the air, she was surprised to get not so much as a blink from the young hostess dressed in a cream-colored suit. And to her further surprise, a scattering of jeans-clad customers dotted the room.

"Welcome to Texas," Ryan whispered by her side, his hand touching her elbow as he guided her through the clusters of elegant white-and-cream decorated tables, in pursuit of the hostess. The touch shimmered up her arm, and spread warmth across her chest.

"I think I could get used to this," she said, the intimacy of his understanding her private insecurities and what she was thinking not escaping her.

The hostess waved them forward, her gaze slipping appreciatively over Ryan as she departed; if he noticed he didn't react. Ryan and Sabrina were greeted by an attractive thirtysomething blonde who quickly stood, displaying a slim figure dressed in a silk blouse and black jeans.

"Ryan, hi," she said. "Glad you came along." And though the words rang genuine, she quickly turned to Sabrina. "Sabrina." She extended her hand. "So very nice to meet you. I'm Calista Montey. And a fan. A huge fan."

"Thank you," Sabrina said, shaking Calista's hand across the table. "I'm always honored to hear someone has enjoyed my work." Which was true. Her column had been her pride and joy, and it had been hard to walk away from it. The fights with her father were another story—a thought that coiled tension in her stomach.

"You clearly stand up for what you believe in," Calista said. "I admire that. I wish more people were like you." She motioned to the chairs. "Please. You two sit down."

Ryan held out Sabrina's chair, a perfect gentleman, something she would expect from a military man. But it was the soft touch of his hand on her back, just so, the silent comfort it offered, followed by a for-her-eyes-only look that said "say no, it's okay," that she found remarkable. As was the invisible blanket of awareness between them she'd never felt in quite this way.

He claimed his chair, and she settled her napkin in her lap. A waiter quickly appeared, and both Sabrina and Ryan ordered coffee, declining food. He was apparently as much of a coffee addict as she was, which she probably found far too appealing for such a little thing.

"We ate right before we talked to you on the phone," Ryan explained to Calista, sticking to the story they'd decided on in the car. They'd eat later, when this was over.

"I'm just glad you were able to join me," Calista chimed quickly. She glanced at Sabrina. "I really appreciate you taking the time to chat with me."

"Chatting is great," Ryan interjected. "But we need some clarification up front. Sabrina left the *Prime* and politics back in New York. She doesn't want where she's living to get spread all over the media. We need your word right here and now that her identity and location stays at this table unless she agrees otherwise."

Sabrina's stomach fluttered at the unfamiliarity of Ryan's protectiveness. It felt nice having someone else stand up for her. And to think she'd believed he might have a political agenda.

Calista's gaze settled heavily on Sabrina. "You..." She looked dumbstruck. "...you left the *Prime*? I mean I knew you'd been gone a few weeks, but I assumed it was vacation. When Ryan said you wanted to interview my brother, I, in turn, assumed you were visiting, that you happened to cross his path and conjured up some political twist to a sports theme."

"No," Sabrina said. "No political twist. My idea for your brother is all about that wildly popular sport of his."

"So you're really gone from the *Prime*? No more politics?"

Sabrina nodded tersely and Calista asked, "Wasn't your column extremely popular?"

"I was blessed with a loyal following, yes," she conceded.

"Then why leave?"

"It's complicated," Sabrina said awkwardly, thankful the coffee attendant appeared just then, disrupting Calista's scrutinizing stare.

Ryan reached under the table and squeezed Sabrina's hand, silencing her. "We need that promise, Calista. Nothing goes beyond this table."

Calista cut Ryan a short look. "Yes, okay. I promise." Her gaze quickly flickered back to Sabrina. "This is about the rumors that your father is going to bid on the presidency, isn't it? He can't have his daughter writing open editorials destroying the policies he stands behind. If his own daughter doesn't believe in him, who will?"

"Like I said," Sabrina repeated, "it's complicated."

Ryan handed her the sugar, which she gladly accepted. Somehow, caffeine and sugar seemed appropriate right now.

"Did your father force you out of the spotlight?"

"No," Sabrina said, quick to purge that idea, irritated to have to battle such speculation, and wondering how many other people would make the same assumption. "I made the decision for myself." And she meant that. Mostly.

Calista looked as if she might question further but changed her mind. "Your column was brave," she said, her voice filled with obvious admiration. "It inspired people to listen to an agenda that isn't politically driven, but people-driven. You spoke your mind no matter who—your father included—might disagree. That's what change is really all about."

"Change will require a complete overhaul of our system," Sabrina said. "My input was a bleep on the neverending screen of the political dysfunction embraced by some of those working inside it."

"Unless your father is running for President."

Discomfort twitched through Sabrina, partially because of the truth in Calista's statement. Her mind chased a memory: she'd been at a party with her parents, talking to her father. A staunch supporter of her father's had waited until she was alone and then proceeded to tell her she was ruining her father's career. He'd insisted that unless she stepped down from her position at the *Prime*—something her parents, despite frequent conflicting opinions, would never ask her to do—her father would not get the nomination for his party.

"You know, Calista," Ryan said dryly, his voice snapping Sabrina out of the past and back to the present as he continued. "Probing Sabrina about things she doesn't want to talk about isn't exactly the way to convince her to..."

"Speak of this event we're having. Sorry, Sabrina," Calista said, having the good grace to be apologetic. "I shouldn't have pushed. Please know it's because I'm a fan, and letting go of your column must have been painful. I was certain your interest in my brother had some political angle."

"Just pure racing bliss for the fans, I hope," Sabrina clarified.

"Why don't you explain to Sabrina what it is you want her to do, Calista," Ryan suggested, ever the one to get right to the point. A quality Sabrina decided could grow on her quite rapidly.

"Right," Calista said. "The city council is organizing a political-ideas discussion, all parties, commentators, journalists will be invited. And I'd be honored if you would consider speaking."

A part of Sabrina burned to say yes to the invitation—this was familiar territory. Who didn't want to feel as if they were valued? Appreciated? She wanted to do good things, to stand up for people, but she didn't know how to do that, and really make a difference. No, she'd hit an emotional wall over the constant conflict her involvement created. She'd made her decision, and she knew she needed a change, at least, until she figured out how, and if, she could contribute in a positive way.

Resolve formed. "As much as I am flattered by your invitation, there is no doubt such an event would pluck me from the obscurity I've come here to find. I can't let that happen."

"You know I want to pressure you," Calista said.

"But you won't," Ryan said firmly, casting Calista a meaningful look. "And that's wonderful of you." His cell rang before he finished the last word.

"Realtor," he told Sabrina after a quick inspection

of the phone. "I'll take this outside." He dismissed himself. Sabrina watched him leave, warmed by his brawny protectiveness. She had friends who'd defended her work at the *Prime*, her editor Ava being one of them. But Ryan's protectiveness wasn't about her work, it was about her.

"From politics to extreme sports, I see," Calista commented. Sabrina refocused on the other woman as Calista sipped her coffee and winked. "I guess I see why you want out of politics."

Had she been drinking her coffee, Sabrina would surely have choked. Playing coy, she pretended they were talking about Calista's brother, Marco. "I wasn't aware race-car driving was considered extreme sports."

"No," Calista agreed. "But jumping out of an airplane with that man sure was. I don't know how I got talked into that. Have you tried it?"

"No," Sabrina said. "I came close but thankfully, you and Marco showed up that day."

"Your luck was my loss," Calista said. "I wish I had a little luck so I could talk you into speaking at my event." She waved off the comment, silently letting Sabrina know she wasn't pressuring her. "Back to the extreme sport otherwise known as Ryan Walker. I'm pretty sure you can come up with some exhilarating activities with that man that do not include skydiving. Don't let him talk you into it." A slow smile slid onto her lips. "He's hot, girl, and he looks at you like he wants to gobble you right up."

"No," Sabrina said dismissively, and then because she

couldn't help herself, leaned forward and asked softly, "He does?"

"Oh, yeah," Calista assured her. "What a way to leave the political white collars behind in style. And honey, with a man like that all to yourself, I don't blame you for wanting to protect your privacy."

Sabrina bit her lip. "This isn't about Ryan."

Calista offered a coy look of her own. "Maybe not," she said. "But I wouldn't blame you if it was." She reached into her purse and slid a card to the table. "Listen, the paper is only a few blocks from my office. We should have lunch. A real lunch, no politics. Just friends."

The two of them would never manage "no politics," which was why Sabrina accepted the card and said nothing but, "Thank you. That would be nice."

"Translation," Calista said knowingly, "no, thanks."

"It's not you," Sabrina said. In fact, she felt she quite clicked with Calista. And that was the problem. "I really need a clean break from politics, and you're clearly immersed in that world."

"I'm not going to talk you into speaking, am I?"

"No," Sabrina agreed. "You're not."

Calista pursed her lips. "I respect that, but I'm still hoping you'll change your mind."

It wasn't long until Ryan returned and did what appeared to come naturally—got right to the point. "So, Calista. How about calling Marco and telling him to give Sabrina her interview?"

"Of course," Calista agreed. "I never meant to have this be some sort of quid pro quo. If Marco made it seem otherwise, I'll happily kick his backside."

Ah, sibling love, Sabrina thought, with wistful amusement. She'd never experienced it, but often thought a friend for life who she could always count on would be a joy.

"Then you won't mind calling Marco now, I assume," Ryan commented. It wasn't a question.

Calista shook her head and glanced at Sabrina. "Did I mention I never jumped out of that plane? He pushed me."

"I encouraged you," Ryan corrected, and gave Sabrina a sideways mischievous look that said the word *push* might be the most accurate.

Calista scoffed and retrieved her cell from her purse. "I felt a distinct push. Like now. Only this time I don't mind. I'm calling Marco."

Several minutes later, Sabrina had not only bypassed Marco's manager and set a time for her phone interview with Marco, but also one with his lead mechanic. She was on the way to her six-week exposé. Now, she just needed Frank's thumbs-up.

Sabrina and Ryan said their goodbyes to Calista and laughed their way across the parking lot. "Tell me you didn't really push Calista out of the plane?"

"Nudged is more like it," Ryan said, yanking open the door to his shiny blue Dodge Ram. "Marco had just told me we'd go by your place if there was time before his flight. I made sure we had time."

His hands settled on her waist, and she stepped onto the ledge to climb inside the truck when a moment of spontaneity hit her. She turned and faced him, her hand resting on his chest, their bodies so very close.

"Thank you," she said, and wrapped her arms around his neck.

"For what?"

"For having no political agenda," she said. "When this Calista thing came up I was afraid…" *that you were like so many before you,* she added silently, but said instead, "…you might have an agenda of your own." His arm wrapped around her waist, folding her into his body.

"Politics is the last thing on my mind where you're concerned." His lips pressed to the corner of hers in a tease of a kiss before sliding full on, where he lingered. Every nerve in her seemed to splinter and then collide into one center point before shimmering through her body. And, for the first time in a very long time, politics was the last thing on her mind. She might just be developing a love for extreme sports. Or at least the one named Ryan.

9

"THIS REALLY ISN'T going to work for me," Ryan said, his tone uncompromising.

Sabrina blinked at Ryan's words, taken aback by how fast and certain his decision appeared.

Leaning against the cherrywood cabinetry of one of five houses the Realtor had shown them over the course of the afternoon, Sabrina watched as Scott Miller, said Realtor in question, tried to hide his impatience. The man might come off as country in his cowboy boots and jeans, as did so many Texans, but Scott was all about business. After five houses, all of which had had charm and appeal, Ryan had quickly dismissed every one as easily as this one. Sabrina was beginning to think she was never going to get Ryan alone to move past their hands-off policy.

"Maybe if you could give me more specifics about what you like or don't like, I'd be able to narrow the search," Scott suggested.

So far Ryan's comments had included "Not for me,"

"Not the one," "Can't see me in this one" and now "This really isn't going to work for me."

"I like the cabinets," Sabrina said, running her finger over the gray-and-maroon granite top and trying to give the Realtor something to go on. "Do you like these, Ryan? Or did you prefer the lighter wood in the last house?"

Ryan shrugged. "They're nice," he said, not indicating which of the two kinds of cabinets he preferred.

Sabrina indicated the floor. "And this is amazing hardwood." The color was light with darker streaks to match the cabinets. "Really gorgeous."

"It's hickory," Scott quickly said.

"Really?" Sabrina said. "I've not heard of hickory hardwoods. I like this quite a lot."

"Big backyard," Ryan said, walking to the sliding glass doors off the casual dining area. "Not sure what I'd do with it. But it's big."

He'd dismissed two prior houses because the yards were too small. Scott's lips thinned with frustration, and really, Sabrina couldn't blame him.

"Since the house is vacant," Sabrina asked, "Can Ryan and I stay and look around? Maybe we can talk through what he likes and doesn't like and narrow the search."

"Absolutely," Scott agreed quickly, and before Sabrina knew it, she was given instructions for locking up and left alone with Ryan, who still stood at that window, staring into the backyard.

Sabrina stared at his aloof form and frowned. There

was always a raw untamed energy to Ryan, but now, it was darker. Almost solemn. Sabrina found herself moving toward him, eager to find out what was going on in his head, in his heart. She felt oddly comfortable with a man she'd just met. A man who somehow felt amazingly familiar. She liked him. Liked him in a way you did an instant friend, with the added perk of intense sexual need. He was a man worth being a little daring for.

She stopped, sliding her arms around him from behind, and hugged him, resting her head on his back. "One might think you really don't want to buy a house."

He turned around and wrapped her in his embrace, offering her the first smile since they'd met that didn't quite reach his eyes. "If you ever take me shopping, I promise not to complain when you try on the entire store," he teased.

She found the idea of big, sexy Ryan sitting outside a dressing room while she tried on clothes a bit disconcerting. And appealing.

Lacing her fingers with his, he led her to the kitchen. "It's nice," he said, releasing her hand and surveying the counters and stainless-steel appliances.

"It's gorgeous," Sabrina said. "It makes the house."

"Not that I cook," he said.

"Well, neither do I," she admitted. "My mother was always so busy, we ate a lot of takeout. Thus I eat a lot of takeout. Or microwave meals. But still. There's something about a great kitchen that makes a home."

He frowned at that. “So, your condo…did it feel like home when you first saw it?”

She nodded and leaned on the counter next to him. “I was in love with it right away. But no, it didn’t feel like home. It felt like someplace I could make home. But I’m drawn to condo-style living because I grew up in Manhattan, where a building, rather than a house, is the norm. Maybe think about what was ‘home’ to you in the past. It’s clearly not the style of the houses we’ve been looking at.”

He scoffed and crossed his arms in front of his chest. “I’ve been in deserts and jungles for so many years, the hotel I’m in feels more like home than this. Though I like your place.” His eyes took on familiar mischief. “But then it might have been the mud mask that turned me on to it.”

Sabrina rolled her eyes. “Can we vow to replace that memory with one that is mud-free?”

“Oh, no,” he said, a teasing, erotic hitch to his voice. “That is a memory I will cling to with immense pleasure, for quite possibly the rest of my life.”

She might have ignored the bold comment, but she couldn’t shake the feeling that Ryan wasn’t himself right now. Not that she knew him well enough to say that, but yet… He joked. He teased. And still he was more withdrawn than normal.

Sabrina eased in front of him and let her body rest against his. Instantly, his eyes darkened, turned an amber-brown. The heat of his body radiated into hers like the soft glow of a newly lit furnace.

Blinking up at him, she wanted to ask him what was wrong, but the newness of their relationship held her back. And so she decided perhaps she should simply give him something else to think about. An escape, pleasure.

"This house might not be home," she offered, her hand sliding across his chest and down his side, "but it's a good place for a memory. And if I remember a certain stairwell properly, I do owe you a memory." Her hand slid over his belt, down the front of his jeans.

His face hardened with desire, and that wasn't the only thing hard. He covered her hand where it rested on his zipper. "You're tempting the beast," he teased, though his voice was taut, his cock hard against her palm.

She surprised herself by laughing. "The one in your pants or out?" she joked playfully, remarkably relaxed with Ryan, even when pushing her own boundaries. And she was very much about to push her boundaries.

"Both," he said. "Man and beast want you way too badly to be teased."

"No teasing," she said, mercilessly stroking him through his jeans. "We've already established I owe you a memory. I intend to pay up." She reached for the snap on his jeans.

Again he stilled her hand, his expression serious, his voice, as well. "You don't owe me anything but a date," he said.

His words stilled her for a moment. She owed him nothing. "Then this is for me," she said. "A memory I want very much." And she did. More than she'd ever imagined possible. She wanted to pleasure this man as she had never wanted to pleasure another. Wanted to forget the world around her. Forget prim and proper. Wanted just to enjoy him here and now.

For several seconds, he held on to her hand, studying her, probing her expression. "I want this," she whispered, using her free hand to shove his shirt upward, to press her fingers against the warm flesh beneath the shirt, to absorb rippling muscles with wonder and delight.

His hand eased from hers, and she unzipped his pants, her fingers quickly finding the hard length of him beneath. She wasn't sure who inhaled the sharpest when she pressed beneath his underwear and grazed his cock with her fingers. Her gaze jerked to his, the connection scorching, intimate, erotic. As was the moment she freed him, closing her palm around his hot pulsing flesh and then stroking slowly up his length, spreading the dampness there, the sign of just how ready he was for what came next.

He moaned, and desire burned wild inside her. Without any hesitation, any fear of being caught, she slid to her knees, arms wrapped around Ryan's legs as she settled beneath his jutted cock and touched it lightly with her tongue. Teasing. Yes. Now she was teasing. Him and herself.

"Sabrina," he whispered.

She smiled as her hand slid around the base of his erection. As her eyes met his, she drew him into her mouth, suckled the head of his erection and then slowly slid downward, inch by inch. And then she started the slide, up and down. Until his hand settled on her head, guiding her, telling her how urgent he was. Until she couldn't get enough, until her hand curved his amazing backside, and she suckled him harder and deeper.

He moaned her name, his breathing heavy, labored. Aroused.

Sabrina had never wanted a man to submit his pleasure to her as she did this one. Never hungered for more of him. But she did now. Her tongue, lips and hands explored, pumped, drove him to the edge. She ached with want, with need, her womb contracting, begging to be filled. Later, she told herself. *Later,* when she could have all of him without restriction, without limitations. Always there were limitations. She wanted them gone, wanted to find out what that meant with this man. What making love really could be. How erotic. How intense. How daring.

Suddenly, the muscles in Ryan's legs stiffened, and his body shuddered. "Stop," Ryan said, trying to pull back, to pull away from her.

Sabrina refused, tightening her grip around him and sucking him deeper, harder. She stole his resistance, his resolve, until his hand slid back to her head, holding her, begging her not to stop. Until finally he exploded, finally he gave himself to her.

Afterward, she slid up his body, helping him dress as he had done with her. And then she settled against him again, a smile tugging at her lips. Gone was the darkness she'd seen edging his face, replaced with a sense of awe and satisfaction that she was responsible for. She loved that she'd done that for him. And for her. She wasn't thinking about who was watching, or who was judging, or what she'd left behind in New York. She was thinking about the moment and, most definitely, about the man.

She reached up and fingered the straight hair touching his brow. She liked that it was longer than a typical army buzz cut. Her hand slid over his strong jaw, the spiky stubble rough against her soft palm. "Now," she prodded, "what do you think about the house?"

His arms held her at the waist. "All I'm thinking about right now is you." The loud growl of her stomach interrupted, and he chuckled, "And you're thinking about food. Not sure how I feel about that."

"A few bites of a muffin doesn't go very far," she said.

"We should go eat, then." His hand slid around her neck, his lips hovering above hers. "I wouldn't want to leave you unsatisfied."

She smiled, again amazed at how comfortable Ryan made her feel. "I'm counting on it."

10

NOT LONG AFTER TURNING the house for sale into the house he'd never forget, Ryan and Sabrina had swung through the Taco Cabana drive-through for takeout. Feeling at ease with Sabrina beyond what he'd expect considering the length of time they'd known one another—like a close friend with the perk of finding her smoking-hot, of course—Ryan now lounged on her living-room floor with her by his side. The final bits of their dinner sprawled across her coffee table, the radio emitted a low hum of country music at Ryan's insistence—Mexican food required proper atmosphere.

Sabrina fanned her mouth and reached for her large diet soda. "I thought you said this was mild," she complained, hitting the icy bottom of her drink and grabbing his to take a long gulp. She set it down with a hard thud. "Good grief. This food is not even close to mild."

Ryan chuckled, finding her inability to tolerate even

the mildest spice adorable and appalling. "You will never make it in Texas if you don't learn to spice things up."

"If spicing up my life includes setting my mouth on fire," she rebutted, and drew another long drink of his soda, "I'm going to reconsider."

"You certainly did the food justice for someone who doesn't like it," he commented.

She looked offended. "You were trying to starve me. I took what I could get."

"You'll be surprised how it'll grow on you," he assured her. "You'll miss it when you're gone."

"If all goes well with this Marco interview," she said hopefully, "I won't be going anywhere to miss it. I really appreciate you getting me the interview."

He helped her gather the trash, stuffing it into a take-out bag and setting it aside. "Completely self-serving," he confessed. "I wanted to see you again, and I had a feeling if you left the Hotzone without jumping, you wouldn't be back to try it again."

She curled her legs to her chest, the silky strands of her hair draped over her slender shoulders. Her ears strained toward the George Straight song "Amarillo by Morning." "This song isn't so bad," she said. "Country music is just such sad music."

"If a song makes you sad, then it's talking to you," he said. "That's what country music is all about. It's thinking music. Well, and drinking and dancing."

"You had me at thinking and drinking," she said. "Lost me at dancing." She grabbed the bag of trash and stood up, doing a catlike stretch that Ryan gave considerable male regard.

On his feet now, he captured her hand in his, using the other to set the food bag on the table. "I think we'll be better off skipping the thinking and drinking," he said, "and getting right to the dancing."

Her eyes went wide. "What?" She shook her head. "No. Ryan. I don't dance."

He led her to the open area in between the television and the couch. "Good thing I do, then," he murmured, sliding his hand to her waist. "Just follow my lead."

"I'll step on your feet," she insisted, a lift to her voice that bordered on genuine concern.

He slid his hands to her cheeks and kissed her. "That's why they make boots." Leaning back, he glanced down at her dainty feet before giving her a grin. "And don't worry. I won't step on your pretty pink toes." A Kenny Chesny song had begun playing, a fast-paced, fun dance tune. Ryan eased her into motion, ignoring her objections. "Here we go. Step. Step. Good. One, two, three. Just follow me, and keep your spine stiff. Step. Step. One, two, three." His hand slid to her backside. "Don't shake that cute little butt of yours. Not for the two-step. Better. Good."

"I am so not good at this."

"You are doing great."

"Because you are really, really good at this," she said. "You're doing it for me."

"Had a lot of years of practice," he said, gently guiding her.

"In the jungles or the deserts?"

"You'd be surprised at where a little piece of Texas shows up," he said.

The music shifted to a slow Keith Urban song. The mood shifted with it, the air suddenly thicker, charged with an expanding awareness. Ryan closed the small space between them, let his hips guide her movements. His chest was tight, his groin with it. He had no doubt she could feel the hard press of his arousal.

She was petite and soft, and he wanted nothing more than to strip away the barriers and hold her in his arms. To feel her on every possible intimate level. But he'd given Sabrina the power to control when, how, and if they were ever to make love. Nothing about what had transpired between them today changed that decision. No matter how much he might want it to.

"Maybe this dancing thing isn't so bad, after all," she murmured.

"Thatagirl," he offered approvingly. "Before you know it, I'll have you jumping out of a plane."

"Oh, no," she said quickly. "That idea was a momentary bleep of insanity that I won't be having again anytime soon."

They'd shifted into a slow sway, barely a dance. "Something made you think you wanted to skydive."

Her lashes lowered, her answer coming slowly. "It's complicated."

"Ah," he said. "Complicated. That's what you said to Calista. In other words…you don't want to talk about it."

She stopped moving, her expression animated, distressed. The lights were dim, but he could see the flush across her cheeks. "No," she said. "That's not what I meant, Ryan. I don't mind talking to you. In fact, you're easy to talk to. The truth is...I thought I was a control freak. I thought jumping out of a plane would teach me to let go, to just live a bit. Or Jennifer thought it would."

"And now you've changed your mind?" he asked, his hand covering hers where it rested on his chest.

"Yes," she said. "Or no. I don't know. It's confusing. I think..." She paused, her delicate brow dipping in consideration, before she continued, "I think I just need to feel like my decisions are my own. That the control I have is not conceived from a need to stay within certain boundaries. I wish I could be more like you. Without boundaries, without fear of what might go wrong." Her fingers curled on his chest, her chin lifting as she stared up at him, vulnerability and insecurity in her eyes, but her voice didn't falter. "I want you to show me what it feels like to let go, Ryan. I want you to..." A knock sounded on the door. Loudly. Over and over.

Silently Ryan cursed, hanging on her words. She wanted him to what? Another knock. Damn it.

"That would be the kid next door who always knocks as though there is a fire or something," she explained, the moment lost as her tone turned matter-of-fact. Gone was the soft, wistful tone of seconds before. She grimaced. "I don't know how I thought he was you when you were you."

Ryan frowned. “What?”

“Nothing,” she said, waving off the question. “He’s persistent. Let me go buy his candy and send him on his way.” She pushed to her toes and kissed Ryan. “Don’t forget where we were.”

Trying to escape, she didn’t get far—Ryan pulled her to him, ignoring the renewed knocking, and kissed her solidly on the lips. “Don’t *you* forget where we were.”

His reward was a beaming, seductive smile. “Oh, I won’t,” she said. “You can count on it.”

Together they walked to the door. “And this kid usually wants what?” he asked.

“For me to buy whatever he is selling.”

Ryan reached for his pocket. “I’ll buy his whole stock if he’ll let us get back to what we were doing.”

Looking amused, Sabrina reached for the door. “I’m sure you are about to make his year.”

Ryan wiggled an eyebrow. “I aim to please,” he said. “Keep that in mind.”

The door opened to reveal a tall, lanky kid, maybe fourteen, with dark-rimmed glasses, holding a package. The kid glanced at Ryan, a stunned look on his face, as if he had hoped to find Sabrina alone. Ryan knew how the kid felt. He wanted her alone, too.

“Hi, Kelvin,” Sabrina said. “Whatcha got for me tonight?”

“Hi, Sabrina,” Kelvin said, casting her a smitten look—if Ryan had ever seen a boy look smitten. But hey. He couldn’t blame the kid on that either. The last time he was as smitten as he was for Sabrina, he’d been fourteen himself and had just moved into his third foster home. That's when he'd met Laurie Monroe, the blonde, big-breasted bombshell of an eighteen-year-old next door, who'd showed him her bare breasts. He'd been her biggest fan until he'd turned sixteen and figured out the hands-on action of Twister rather than the hands-off game of show-and-tell.

"The mailman left this package for you at our house," Kelvin said. "It came yesterday. I would have brought it sooner, but we went out of town last night. I had a band competition."

Sabrina accepted the oversize square package, and Ryan took it from her. "Well, thank you so much for doing this, Kelvin," she said. "How'd you fare at the competition?"

Kelvin straightened with pride. "First Place District."

"Yay!" Sabrina said, clapping. "How exciting." She hugged Kelvin, and Ryan captured a glimpse of the boy's expression.

Ryan barely stifled a chuckle before the door shut, allowing him to let it fully rip. "You almost gave that boy a cardiac arrest at a tender, too-young age."

Sabrina's brow dipped. "What are you talking about?"

They moved toward the living room as Ryan replied, "You can't possibly be oblivious to the lovestruck-puppy eyes he gives you."

"He's a kid, Ryan!" she protested.

"He's a teenage boy," Ryan corrected. "That's a whole different breed."

"That's crazy," she said, dismissing the idea. "He's so cute." She sat down on the couch. "And sweet."

"And hormonal," he added. Ryan set the package on the coffee table and joined her on the couch.

Sabrina instantly reached for the package. "No return address. Hmm. I'm curious now." She ripped open the outside paper.

Ryan balled it up and snatched the food bags. "Trash can in the kitchen, I assume?"

"Pantry by the stove," she said, removing the paper on the outside of the box. "Thank you."

Whistling, Ryan headed to the kitchen, admiring the city lights through the expanse of windows wrapping around the room. He was at ease in a way he couldn't imagine himself ever feeling in one of the houses he'd viewed today. Maybe he needed a condo. Maybe he just needed Sabrina. It was an off-the-wall thought, and he dismissed it. Ryan opened the pantry door, quickly disposed of the trash and then stared at the shelves in disbelief. Rows of food were organized in perfect lines.

Ryan scrubbed his jaw. "You'd think she was the one who'd been in the military for fourteen years," he murmured to himself. She most definitely had some control issues. It was going to be interesting to see who played the submissive in bed. Maybe they'd take turns.

With that thought in mind, Ryan made a fast return to the living room. Instantly, Ryan noted the crackling silence in the air, coupled with the look on Sabrina's face as she appeared absorbed in the pages of what looked like a photo album or perhaps a scrapbook.

Ryan hesitated to approach, pausing, taken aback by more than her mood. She was beautiful, classy and elegant in a way that defied her Harley T-shirt and jeans. The type of woman who comfortably rubbed shoulders with Washington types—the types who sent guys like himself out into the scary places of the world to swim through blood and death.

Seeming to sense his attention, she glanced up from the book. "It's from my father," she said, a distinct tinge of bitterness to her tone. "A scrapbook of highlights of my career."

Ryan joined her but said nothing, watching her thumb through stories. She laughed at one and showed him the photo of a man with a pie in his face. "I got in a lot of trouble for this one."

"You threw the pie?" he teased, hoping to coax a smile. "Remind me not to piss you off."

She granted him the smile he'd hoped for. "No. I didn't throw the pie. But I did suggest that anyone who voted for a certain bill—I won't bore you with its content—had pie in their face and would feel the effects at the voting booths. My father showed up at the newspaper the morning it ran."

Realization hit Ryan. "He voted for the bill."

She nodded and he asked, "And you knew?"

Her smile faded. "I knew. He had his reasons. We disagreed on those reasons being valid. He had a problem with me voicing that disagreement. Said it was a personal attack when it wasn't. The fight that ensued was hurtful and got as much attention as the article itself."

Ryan studied her carefully. "So why exactly did your father send you a copy of that particular column?"

She grabbed the note lying on the couch and read, "Together we can show the world the beauty of disagreeing. We can cross party lines and change the world. Come home. You are missed and needed." She dropped the card. "He changed his vote after all was said and done."

"Because of you?"

"Because of public opinion," she said. "Which I helped rally, but that's not the point. The point now is someone on his campaign team has decided I can somehow help him win the election rather than the opposite. Or perhaps that my silence can be used for ammunition as easily as my speaking out. That's the only way to explain the sudden support."

"He could really miss you," he said.

She looked at the front and back of the note. "Don't see that anywhere on the paper. Not from my father or my mother, who was quick to approve of me leaving the *Prime*."

Ryan questioned her a little about her mother, learning about her job as a professor, her support of her husband's White House vision, before she added. "Don't get me wrong. My parents love me. I know that. It's just… the White House comes first. It's bigger than me." She shut the book. "This package is about strategy." She set the book on the table and turned to him. "I'm so glad to be away from that world." Her hand slid to his leg. "I really need to be away from it. I need to forget it."

Her hand inched up his leg. Turbulent emotions splintered off her like shattered glass, spreading through the room with prickly warning. Anything she did right now was born of that emotion, not of sound judgment.

Ryan stared at her as she inched closer, her hand creeping farther up his leg, the floral scent of woman and desire threading his nostrils. He wanted her. He wanted her in a bad way. This was a woman he could fall for. It was a hard realization, as was the fact that she wanted an escape, not him. Points near impossible to absorb beyond pure lust as she pressed herself close to his side, her lip brushing his jaw. Her hand farther up his thigh. She wasn't running from him this time. She was running from her past.

Ryan knew what that meant… it meant regret. And that wasn't what he wanted from Sabrina. Normally, he'd say "Hell, yeah" to such an arrangement. Hell, yeah to a voluptuous, sexy woman who would be happy with a fast goodbye. But there was nothing normal about the way Sabrina had climbed inside him and taken hold. And just then, climb she did, shocking him as she slid across his lap to straddle him.

His hands went to her slender waist. Her arms wrapped around his neck. The V of her body hugged his rock-hard erection, and desire ripped through his body. She leaned forward to kiss him, her breasts high and close, begging for his hands.

Somehow, Ryan pulled back. Somehow, he reminded himself she wasn't thinking straight. "What are you doing, Sabrina?"

"I don't want to wait, Ryan," she purred. "I want you. I want you now." Her mouth had somehow moved closer again. Her breath warm.

"What happened to all that reserve you were showing?" he asked, his voice rougher than intended, laden with burning need.

"I thought this was what you wanted," she purred, ignoring the question. "I thought you wanted me." The witch shifted slightly over his hips, rubbing herself against his erection. He wanted her moving like that with nothing between them. He wanted to feel her wet and hot, wrapped around him. Riding him.

Her mouth pressed to his, soft and full of promise. Ryan felt the touch in every inch of his body, told himself to stop. Told himself just one more second. And another. Her tongue was what did him in. It flickered against his lips and sent a surge of need through him.

Ryan's hand slid to the back of her head, threaded through her silky hair and pulled her mouth fully to his. Tasted her. Drank her. Hungered for more, for all of her. Soft moans slid from her mouth, feeding that need. He touched her. Exploded. Her shirt came off, and she tossed it aside. Somehow, in the act, the book fell to the floor. The thud wasn't loud, but it rumbled through Ryan with an impact.

Sabrina reached for the front clasp of her bra, and Ryan pulled her to him, hugging her, inhaling her scent and drinking in a hard dose of sanity. The book. The damn book that had started this. The book, symbolic of how different her world was from his. How he and Sabrina, somehow together now, in a moment in time, were just that—a moment in time.

He was, like the Mexican food, a walk in the unusual for her. An adventure. A memory she may or may not even claim. And for reasons Ryan couldn't explain, that idea dug at his consciousness. Gnawing away at him inside and out. He told himself to use her. That she was using him as so many before her had done, while he was here today. He might be gone tomorrow. But Sabrina wasn't like the others, and why that was, he didn't know, nor did it matter because this was going nowhere. Because she was acting out of character, and she would hate him for doing this tomorrow. And she'd hate him now for stopping her, but nevertheless, he had to end this.

With almighty will, Ryan set her away from him. "No," he said. She gasped, her breath coming out in hard blasts. He pushed to his feet, ran a hand over his face and then over his neck. "Not like this. You want me because I'm some sort of statement. Some sort of payback. Which is exactly why I should take you up on your offer and enjoy myself and not look back." He snatched her shirt and tossed it to her. "But I won't do that."

She looked down, inching her arms into her shirt,

unwilling to make eye contact. No denial. No vow she wanted him. Not so much as a word. Her silence was the final dig with that ice pick. Ryan ran his hand over his face again and headed to the door, no saunter in sight. His step was fast, as was his exit, sealed with a promise of goodbye.

GET 2 BOOKS

We'd like to send you two *Harlequin® Blaze®* novels absolutely free. Accepting them puts you under no obligation to purchase any more books.

HOW TO GET YOUR 2 FREE BOOKS AND 2 FREE GIFTS

1. Return the reply card today, and we'll send you two *Harlequin Blaze* novels, absolutely free! We'll even pay the postage!
2. Accepting free books places you under no obligation to buy anything, ever. Whatever you decide, the free books and gifts are yours to keep, free!
3. We hope that after receiving your free books you'll want to remain a subscriber, but the choice is yours—to continue or cancel, any time at all!

EXTRA BONUS

You'll also get two free mystery gifts! (worth about $10)

FREE!
Return this card today to get
2 FREE BOOKS and 2 FREE GIFTS!
HARLEQUIN® Blaze®
YES! Please send me 2 FREE Harlequin® Blaze® novels, and 2 free mystery gifts as well. I understand I am under no obligation to purchase anything, as explained on the back of this insert.
About how many NEW paperback fiction books have you purchased in the past 3 months?
❑ 0-2 E9RD
❑ 3-6 E9RP
❑ 7 or more E9RZ
151/351 HDL
FIRST NAME
LAST NAME
ADDRESS
APT.#
CITY
STATE/PROV.
ZIP/POSTAL CODE
Visit us at: www.ReaderService.com
Offer limited to one per household and not applicable to series that subscriber is currently receiving. Your Privacy—The Reader Service is committed to protecting your privacy. Our Privacy Policy is available online at www.ReaderService.com or upon request from the Reader Service. We make a portion of our mailing list available to reputable third parties that offer products we believe may interest you. If you prefer that we not exchange your name with third parties, or if you wish to clarify or modify your communication preferences, please visit us at www.ReaderService.com/consumerschoice or write to us at Reader Service Preference Service, P.O. Box 9062, Buffalo, NY 14269. Include your complete name and address.
▼ DETACH AND MAIL CARD TODAY! ▼
(H-B-03/11)

The Reader Service - Here's how it works:

Accepting your 2 free books and 2 free mystery gifts (mystery gifts worth approximately $10.00) places you under no obligation to buy anything. You may keep the books and gifts and return the shipping statement marked "cancel". If you do not cancel, about a month later we'll send you 6 additional books and bill you just $4.24 each in the U.S. or $4.71 each in Canada. That is a savings of at least 15% off the cover price. It's quite a bargain! Shipping and handling is just 50¢ per book in the U.S. and 75¢ per book in Canada.* You may cancel at any time, but if you choose to continue, every month we'll send you 6 more books, which you may either purchase at the discount price or return to us and cancel your subscription.

*Terms and prices subject to change without notice. Prices do not include applicable taxes. Sales tax applicable in N.Y. Canadian residents will be charged applicable taxes. Offer not valid in Quebec. All orders are subject to credit approval. Credit or debit balances in a customer's account(s) may be offset by any other outstanding balance owed by or to the customer. Books received may not be as shown. Please allow 4 to 6 weeks for delivery. Offer valid while quantities last.

If offer card is missing, write to: The Reader Service, P.O. Box 1867, Buffalo, NY 14240-1867 or visit www.ReaderService.com

NO POSTAGE NECESSARY IF MAILED IN THE UNITED STATES

BUSINESS REPLY MAIL

FIRST-CLASS MAIL PERMIT NO. 717 BUFFALO, NY

POSTAGE WILL BE PAID BY ADDRESSEE

THE READER SERVICE
PO BOX 1867
BUFFALO NY 14240-9952

11

"YOU ARE THE MOST amazing woman I've ever met."

It was Friday morning, almost a week after her disastrous attempt to play seductress with Ryan. Sabrina looked up to find her boss Frank standing in her doorway. Seeing him but not really seeing him. Frank was Frank. New version of the same white shirt and black tie, with a smug expression plastered on his well-lined face.

Sabrina, however, had gone for a celebratory outfit today that she'd hoped would be lucky. A red-and-black leather racing jacket and black jeans—the jacket a gift from Calista, probably to shmooze her into a speech—but still appropriate for this day, considering the occasion.

On Sabrina's desk lay the paper featuring her first interview in the six-part series called "An Intimate Ride in Marco Montey's Backseat." Apparently, Frank was pleased with the results. At least she could please someone. It sure wasn't Ryan. In fact, he'd been quite obviously displeased when she'd gone from prim senator's daughter to seductress. She'd dared to reach beyond her comfort zone, and he'd been all about "regrets" and "can't do that," etc. Then he'd run. Exactly why she'd refused his calls—her mother's and father's, too, for that matter, but that was another story—and had worked late every night. Of course, if he'd really wanted to see her, he'd have found a way.

"Jerk," she mumbled.

"Easy now," Frank said dryly, snapping her back to the present. "I've been called a jerk by pretty women plenty of times, but not usually after I tell one she's wonderful."

"Amazing," Sabrina corrected, setting the stage for what she wanted. "You called me amazing."

"Okay," he said. "You're wonderful and amazing. This is where you say 'thank you, Frank.' Or even 'I know.' Or 'told you so.' Not where you call me a jerk."

"Does this mean you'll stop bugging me about attending political functions?"

"If you really want me to," he said. "But check your email. I sent you some interesting tidbits on the soldier-turned-bank robber. Then get to work on part two of the Marco spread. You gave us the Can Cola and Red Rock conflict in story one. Give me something good week two. I expect the phones and email to light up next week, like they are today." He disappeared down the hall.

Frank was elated, and hadn't said a word to her about politics, except for the MIA wife, all week long. *She* should be elated, excited, thrilled to the bone. She was on her way to a new career, a new life. That made it a good day. Good. Day.

She itched to read that email from Frank. Told herself not to. Told herself to object. To have him forward it elsewhere. Her finger was almost on the delete key when the phone on the desk jangled. Sabrina inhaled and stared at the offending device.

She reached for the phone. "This is Sabrina."

"Read the email," Frank ordered and hung up.

Sabrina grimaced and hung up the phone, then opened the email that read, "Look at the date on the attached." She frowned and pressed the key to bring the attachment into view. It was a copy of the mayor's visitation register that showed the wife of the dead soldier visiting him, then another copy of the same document, that had been edited to erase her name. She eyed the date and her jaw dropped. The wife had visited the mayor before her husband had died. What the heck was going on?

She quickly typed an email to a friend in a high place to see what she could find out about the soldier's military unit, and then another to a medical specialist she knew who'd been a credible source in the past. She knew someone well up in the Army ranks, as well, a friend of her father's, but getting him to talk would mean first talking to her father. She'd hold off on that contact as long as she could. She'd barely finished typing the emails when her phone rang again. She grabbed it. "I saw the document," she said, without giving Frank time to talk. "And yes, I'll look into the story further, but I'm only helping, someone else can take any credit. No—I don't, so don't ask."

"I expected *no* after you ignored my calls for a week, but you could at least say hello first," came the warm, sexy, maddening voice so unmistakably Ryan's.

"Funny," Sabrina said before hesitation could form. "I thought you liked the word *no* far more than *yes.*"

"I like *yes* very much," he said, his voice a soft purr of seduction.

She snorted. "Just not from me."

"Most definitely from you."

She could feel her jaw tense. "Right. That's why you left. Because you wanted me."

"I want you, but I want you honest. Not reacting to emotion you may regret the next morning. But that night, things were, as you like to say…complicated. Under the same circumstances, I'd still do the same thing."

Emotions spun inside her and settled in her chest with a thundering jolt. She wanted to see Ryan. She wanted to touch Ryan. She wanted him to want her so much he couldn't walk away like he had. But he didn't. He couldn't. And it upset her on some deep, irrational level that she blamed on some feminine need, bordering on fantasy, to feel desired by a man as ruggedly male as Ryan. That had to be it. There could be no other reason. They barely knew each other.

When she didn't immediately respond, he gave her a reprieve with a lighter subject. "I saw your Marco feature. It's good, Sabrina. Really good."

"Thank you," she said, relieved, the change in topic

allowing her a chance to regroup. "It would never have happened without your help."

"My help wouldn't have mattered if you hadn't turned the interview and the presentation into gold. I'm sure you'll soon have the new career. That is, if you decide you still want it."

Still want it? What did that mean? She would have asked, but he spoke first. "We should talk," he said softly. "In person."

"No," she said quickly when she wanted to say yes. Wanting him more than he wanted her would only mean heartache she couldn't withstand right now. Resolve thickening, she repeated, "No. I think it's better we leave things as they are. I'm a firm believer that things happen for a reason."

Suddenly, Jennifer appeared in her doorway, smiling and waving a hand, looking adorable in jeans and a blue-and-white plaid shirt. She tipped her hand back and pretended to drink, and then mouthed, "Happy hour."

"Sabrina—" Ryan started.

"I have to go," she said. "I've got a visitor. Thanks for calling. It was—" she paused for the right choice of words "—good to hear from you."

She could hear his hesitation, his frustration, crackle through the phone line, before he said, "Goodbye, Sabrina." And the line clicked. Sabrina's stomach pretty much hit the floor at the sound. That was it. She should be relieved. And she would be. Soon.

Sabrina motioned Jennifer forward. "Did someone say happy hour?"

WITH A GRIMACE, Ryan ended the call with Sabrina, his boots scraping off the wooden desk of his Hotzone office where they'd rested. He planted his feet solidly on the ground. Damn it to hell, the woman was killing him. Giving him mental whiplash. Never in his life had he had a woman do this to him. Thank God the Army had contracted a skydiving training camp at the Hotzone—he'd been absorbed with it all week, sunup to sundown. Otherwise, he might have gone and seen Sabrina, and made a real fool of himself. At least he'd got the proverbial "Dear John" slap in the face by phone.

In avoidance mode, Ryan headed to the lobby of the Hotzone, determined not to speak to anyone, feeling fouler than foul and he knew it. But before he made it down the narrow hallway, he heard his name.

It was Bobby, and he could hear Caleb mumbling in the background.

Groaning inwardly, Ryan called over his shoulder. "Whatever it is has to wait. I'm outta here." The last thing he wanted right now was to talk business, which had been all the Aces had been about for a month. Which was cool and all, but not now, not tonight.

"What if we said dollar beer on draft was involved?" Caleb shouted.

Ryan stopped walking. Turned on his heels. "I'd say... what *are* we waiting for?"

SHORTY'S WAS A COUNTRY BAR complete with cowboys, women in tight jeans and lots of loud talking and laughing. Eyeing the couples sashaying around the dance floor near her table, a memory of dancing with Ryan, all close and cozy, assailed her. Why, oh, why, had she agreed to this?

The two-dollar happy-hour margaritas that she and Jennifer had ordered appeared on the table, and Sabrina's eyes lit. "Oh, yeah. That's exactly what I need right now." Sitting at a high wooden table next to Jennifer, she sipped long and deep.

A tall cowboy with sandy-brown hair appeared in front of the table. "Howdy there, ma'am," he said. "Wanna dance?"

Sabrina looked at Jennifer. Jennifer laughed. "He's talking to you."

"Me?" she silently mouthed, and jerked her gaze to his. "Oh, no. No. I mean, thank you, but I came to drink. No dancing."

The guy gazed at her with a bit of a wounded look and then turned tail. "Jeez," Sabrina said. "I need to make a sign that says Unsafe On The Dance Floor."

"What fun is that?" Jennifer said. "Dancing makes the world a better place." She snickered. "Or maybe it's margaritas."

"Hear, hear," Sabrina agreed, taking a big swallow. "And I don't get this 'ma'am' stuff. How is making me feel old going to get me to dance? Or anywhere else for that matter."

"This is Texas, Sabrina," Jennifer said. "*Ma'am* is just part of the culture. It's not about age."

Jennifer's cell phone buzzed with a text message. "Oh, good," she said after reading it, pushing to her feet to wave through the crowd. "Bobby!" He appeared through the crowd and Jennifer motioned him forward before sitting back down. "I've barely seen him all week. The Hotzone just landed a contract to train small groups of soldiers for the Army. The guys worked darn near around the clock all week."

The guys, meaning Bobby, Caleb and Ryan. So Ryan had been consumed all week. A tiny part of Sabrina lit with that news, clinging to an excuse as to why he might not have come by to see her.

Suddenly, Caleb appeared in the crowd, directly behind Bobby, both men striding across the room with that same confident, dominant vibe that Ryan possessed. Sabrina held her breath, wondering if Ryan was about to appear, her heart thundering in her ears.

But Ryan was nowhere to be found. Sabrina told herself it was relief she felt, though the ball in her stomach screamed of disappointment.

Bobby appeared by Jennifer's side and gave her a hug and kiss. Caleb took up command on the opposite side of the table, giving Sabrina a quick "hello" before flagging a waiter. Soon, the beer was flowing, and the laughter with it.

Caleb offered her his hand. "Hi. Caleb. I think we were supposed to jump together, weren't we?"

"The timing wasn't right," Jennifer said. "Ryan was going to take her up for you, but then Marco showed up."

"So when are you coming back out?" Caleb asked.

"I'll take you up." He smiled, friendly rather than flirtatious. "I'm nicer than Ryan."

Probably true, but not more interesting and definitely not hotter. Her cheeks flamed instantly with the thought, and Sabrina quickly sipped her drink and tried to hide the reaction. Then she replied, "I think I'll pass. It was one of those fleeting, daredevil things that I talked myself out of."

Caleb tipped his drink back and studied her. "Ryan didn't scare you away, did he?"

No. She'd scared him away. "Jumping was Jennifer's idea. I shouldn't have listened."

"She's a control freak," Jennifer chimed.

"Ryan would have scared the crap out of you, then," he said, and then frowned, eying Bobby. "Speaking of Ryan. Where is he? He said he was coming."

"He pulled off at the gas station a few miles back," Bobby said. "He'll be here."

"What'd he do?" Caleb asked. "Use a water hose to fill his tank?"

Sabrina felt every nerve-ending in her body come to life. She'd said nothing to Jennifer about Ryan. Told her nothing beyond the ride with Marco. Ryan was her little secret.

"There he is!" Bobby shouted, and then whistled. "Ryan! Over here!"

Sabrina wasn't prepared for this. Hadn't counted on this. She leaned into Jennifer. "Restroom break. Be right back." Sabrina didn't wait for an answer, quickly weaving into the crowd, careful to avoid Ryan's path.

The restroom was behind the DJ booth, on the other side of the room, which was good because it gave her more time to figure out how to get out of this mess. She wasn't up to facing her one-night stand that wasn't really a one-night stand, but a night of embarrassment.

She darted around the corner of the open archway leading to a row of mirrors and chairs. A chair. Oh, yes. Sabrina sank into the faux-leather seat, her knees wobbling.

"You okay, sweetie?" a tall woman in a sparkly T-shirt and tight-fitting jeans asked her, sounding far more motherly than her appearance suggested. "You look like you've seen a ghost…or an ex-boyfriend."

Sabrina tried to smile. "Just a guy with a bad two-step, right onto my feet. Hiding. Hoping he goes away."

The woman chuckled and waved a hand. "Good strategy. Hope it works." She headed for the door, sashaying away, swinging her hips wildly.

One woman after another whisked in and out of the restroom, and Sabrina realized that she couldn't stay here forever. Jennifer would come looking for her. No. She needed to sneak out of the bar and call Jennifer from the car. Make her escape.

Sabrina pushed to her feet and caught a glimpse of herself in the mirror. She barely recognized herself, and it wasn't because her business suit had been traded for black jeans and a black V-neck tank that morning.

She was not her father's daughter here, she realized. And she liked that. Sure, race-car driving didn't excite her. Politics didn't excite her. But the American dream did. People did. Heroes of the people. A soldier who'd once committed to protecting the innocent, but who'd become a bank robber. What caused that? How could it have been prevented? Those were her type of stories. But dang, she thought, straightening, she'd use this feature on Marco to open doors, to find her stories of the heart. She liked that she had her own life. And no one, not even a hot cowboy who'd turned her down when she'd taken a risk with him, was going to stop her.

Sabrina headed to the door. She wasn't sneaking away. She wasn't running. And, never mind that Ryan Walker, she was going to use his dance lessons with everyone but him to prove to him she was resilient. To prove to herself she was truly in control of her own destiny. And no one was going to take that away from her.

12

PULLING BACK HER SHOULDERS, Sabrina marched toward the restroom exit, through the door and barely managed to draw to a halt before barreling into the tall, hard man leaning in an oh-so-casual stance against the wall.

Sabrina silently gulped, refusing to back away despite the too-close-for-comfort proximity. Calling on years of socializing, she enlisted her own oh-so-casual coolness. "Ryan," she said. "I didn't know you were here."

"Liar," he said, reaching for her and bringing her so close they were knee to knee. His hand was big, warm. Her arms tingled to the shoulder. "You ran when you saw me."

"It was my turn," she said, deciding not to hide the truth. "You ran last time." The music saved her from saying more. Like how she'd dared to think he was the guy she could let go with, only to find out he only wanted her when she fitted some ideal he was fantasizing about.

"Yet here we are," he said. "Things happen for a reason, right? It must be a sign."

Sabrina could feel him in every inch of her body, could smell him and even taste him on her tongue. Damn him. She sidestepped him. "It's a sign I need a drink."

He shackled her arm gently, held her by his side, but said nothing, the shadows hiding his eyes, but not their impact. And when she thought he would speak, he simply released her. Sabrina released the breath she'd been unconsciously holding and all but ran back to the table.

HE SAT ACROSS FROM HER, like the hot sun on a Texas day—inescapable, scorching. It was an hour after their restroom-door encounter, and Sabrina—a one-drink kind of girl—was on her third margarita, feeling a buzz in a big way. But she didn't care. She was tired of limits, the kind of limits Ryan swore he helped people push past, yet with her, he'd pulled her back. He'd given her limits like everyone else in her life. She hated him for that. But she still wanted him, infuriatingly so. He sat directly across from her, Caleb by his side, Jennifer and Bobby to her left—the three Aces chatting it up about their training camp at the Hotzone this week. Every time Ryan's eyes found hers, a touch without a touch, invisible sparks crackled in the air so fiercely she thought them impossible to hide. If anyone noticed they didn't comment, but Sabrina thought she caught a knowing glance from Jennifer a few times. No doubt, tomorrow would come with questions.

And no matter how Sabrina tried to absorb herself in chatter of her own with Jennifer, the Aces and Ryan entwined themselves in the conversation.

"That Kris Wilks kid I told you about," Bobby said, grinning, talking mostly to Jennifer. "Ryan scared the holy crap out of him today."

Caleb almost choked on his beer. "Kid thought he was dead when his main chute didn't open."

"You rigged his chute not to open?" Sabrina demanded of Ryan, appalled by such an action.

Caleb didn't seem to notice the question, continuing, "After all that gloating the kid did, talking about being the best, not needing any training, he froze like an icicle. Didn't pull his backup."

"Oh, my God," Sabrina murmured.

"My God, Ryan!" Jennifer exclaimed. "He could have been killed."

Ryan shrugged. "I pulled his chute for him."

Bobby ran his hand over Jennifer's back. "Whoa, tigress. Ryan had his reasons, and they were good ones."

"And it was priceless watching that kid get pulled down a notch," Caleb said. "But, man, he hugged you like he loved you, Ryan."

Sabrina frowned, talking to Ryan. "What if you hadn't got to him on time?"

"He would have died," Jennifer answered for him,

and glared at Caleb and Bobby. "And both of you should be ashamed for backing this."

"That kid learned a lesson with the best parachute he could get," Bobby chimed in. "The manmade kind—an Ace. He won't have an Ace in enemy territory."

"Yeah," Caleb agreed. "Ryan probably saved that kid's life twenty times over. He was arrogant, and without reason. Dangerous to himself and everyone around him." Caleb and Bobby raised their beers to Ryan, and Caleb said, "To saving lives by busting balls."

Sabrina stared at Ryan. He enticed her, turned her on, intrigued her. But she admired him, too, envied him. For living his life. For being daring and adventurous. But there was more to him than daring. Bobby and Caleb respected Ryan. When was the last time she'd sat with a group of people who didn't seem to want more from each other than company? How many of her friends from New York had even called since she left? Called without an agenda?

She trusted him. Everyone at this table trusted each other. *Trust me,* Ryan had said to her, as well. She hadn't realized, until this moment, how much she needed someone to trust. How much Ryan had felt like he could be that person until he'd left her that night. Until she'd opened herself up to him, and he'd turned her away.

Ryan paused with the bottle to his lips, noting her attention. He arched a brow, a silent question in the action. She felt vulnerable under his scrutiny, and cut her gaze. Damn it, he confused her. If they'd had sex, she could blow this off as a fling. An adventure. But they hadn't, and she couldn't.

"What is it about a group of Army guys that requires analogies revolving around male body parts?" Jennifer asked, jerking Sabrina back into the conversation, and adding, "I'm sorry, Sabrina. I'm sure you're used to a more refined group than this. Of course, there is Frank. He has a mouth on him."

"Are you kidding?" Sabrina asked, quite amused by the assumption that she was sheltered. "I'm from New York. Frank is nothing. Us New Yorkers are talkers. And politicians? *Biggest trash talkers ever.* Give them some booze and stand back. It's gonna get ugly."

"Really?" Jennifer mused. "I always thought they kept a straight face in public, and let it all hang out behind closed doors."

The music changed suddenly, transitioning between songs, and Jennifer grabbed Sabrina's arm in excitement. "Oh, wow." Then she turned to Bobby, interrupting whatever he was saying to Caleb. "It's our song. Our song." She shuffled off her seat and tugged Bobby to the dance floor.

A cute blonde came up to Caleb and whispered in his ear. Caleb turned to the woman, chatting with her, angling his body to tune Ryan and Sabrina out of the conversation.

Several crackling seconds of silence passed between Sabrina and Ryan until Ryan eyed her almost-empty glass and then slid to her side of the table. His arm brushed hers, and just that easily, an erotic chill fluttered across her skin. Hot and then cold. Cold and then hot. He turned to face her, elbows on the table.

"One more drink and I might have to drive you home," he commented.

"One more drink and I might need to call a cab," she rebutted.

"Why are you so angry with me?" he asked.

"Why?" she asked and her loosened tongue sped on. "I needed you the other night, and you left me alone." The words fell between them, and she willed them back into her mouth in all their vulnerable clarity.

Ryan's expression softened, and he reached for her. "Sabrina—"

"Caleb!" Sabrina shouted, scooting to the edge of her chair and jerking Caleb's attention from the blonde. "Let's dance!"

RYAN STOOD AT THAT TABLE, watching as Sabrina not only darted away, but snagged Caleb from the blonde he'd been flirting with. She dragged him to the dance floor when she clearly didn't even know how to dance. Ryan ground his teeth, his eyes practically crossing as he watched Caleb's hand settle on Sabrina's waist. Watched her laugh as she tripped on his feet. Caleb, his brother Ace, was holding Sabrina.

Long strides fueled by the agitation vibrating from within, Ryan was on the move. He crossed the bar and nudged onto the dance floor with the insistence of a man on a mission. He tapped Caleb on the shoulder with his last bit of reserve and said, "This would be my dance."

"Hey, man..." Caleb started to object, but the laughter on his lips faded, along with his objection, the instant he looked at Ryan. "Right. Your dance."

"I asked Caleb to dance," Sabrina argued.

Caleb was smart enough to ignore the objection, quickly removing his hands from Sabrina's waist, as if he felt he might lose one of them if he did not. He was right.

Before Caleb had fully backed away, Ryan had hold of Sabrina, pulling her close, his hand around her waist. His legs twined with hers. A slow song fluttered in the air, and Ryan turned her into the crowd, pacing her slowly, controlling her with his hips.

"If you were trying to get a reaction," he said, his hand sliding over her lower back, molding her to him, "it worked." Their lips were close, breath mingling together. "Here I am. Now what are you going to do with me?"

"I wanted to dance," she said, her hand flattening on his chest, applying pressure.

"With Caleb," he challenged.

She hesitated, her lashes fluttering low, shielding her expression. "*We've* already danced," she said. "It didn't go so well."

"Come on, Sabrina," he said, her words steamrolling him, and he pressed his cheek to hers. "I left because I wasn't going to be the jerk who'd taken advantage of you when you woke up the next morning."

She glared up at him. Then he leaned forward to

make sure he could hear her, as she said, "You left the minute I didn't live up to your good-girl, senator's-daughter fantasy."

Instantly, Ryan stilled, his hand sliding behind her neck, pulling her mouth to his. "I left the minute you became the senator's daughter, angry at her father and looking to use me as revenge." Emotions rolled inside him, turbulent, dark. "You know what. You're right. The last dance didn't go well, and neither is this one."

Ryan let her go and started walking, telling himself to go, not to look back. But he stopped, Sabrina's words echoing in his head, *You left me when I needed you.* Damn it to hell. Ryan just stood there, knowing full well he was headed toward heartache.

He turned back to her, finding her staring after him, fraught with the same kind of twisting, turning, confusing emotions he was feeling. Ryan closed the distance and grabbed her, pulling her close.

Sabrina opened her mouth to speak, but the words faded into the steel guitar of a new song. The music was fast now, louder, people two-stepping and twirling around them. That left only one way to communicate.

"Screw discretion," Ryan murmured and kissed her soundly on the lips, slanting his mouth over hers. She clung to him, no hesitation in her response. He damn near made love to her with his mouth right there on the dance floor.

The shift in the music was all that drew him up short. Ryan tore his mouth from hers, searched her face and found no regret, no anger or embarrassment. There was only desire and promise. “Come on,” he said, grabbing her hand and pulling her toward the door.

They were about to hit the exit when suddenly, Sabrina resisted. “Wait. Stop. No. I can’t.”

13

EVEN IN HER SENSUAL HAZE, Sabrina managed one piece of common sense. “My purse is at the table. I have to have my purse.”

Ryan’s tense features softened marginally. “Can’t you get it from Jennifer tomorrow?”

Oh, how she wished, but that wasn’t an option. She shook her head. “My keys are inside. And my cell phone. I’ll be right back.”

He took a step forward, to follow. “No. I’ll go.”

His face flickered with suspicion, and on a whim, she pushed to her toes and kissed him. “I don’t want to risk Jennifer giving us a hard time. I’ll hurry. I promise.”

Reluctantly, he nodded, and she darted away, wobbly enough that she could have used Ryan’s help. To her relief the table was empty, and Sabrina hurried to her chair. Her purse was gone. She searched high and low to no avail. Reality began to creep over the situation. How stupid she’d been.

Ryan appeared, looking concerned.

"It's gone. I'm never letting loose again." She walked over to him and dropped her head to his chest before looking up at him. "I can't believe this is happening. They got my credit cards, my keys. God. Ryan, my ID has my address. And I am so fuzzy-headed, I can't think what to do first. I'm never like this. Never."

He kissed her forehead. It was the most tender, sweet thing a guy had ever done. "You can stay with me tonight," he said. "Tomorrow I'll change your locks for you. But right now we need to report this to the manager."

Caleb walked up and made quick work of helping, flagging a manager. A few minutes later, Sabrina and Ryan stood talking to the manager and an off-duty police officer in a far corner of the bar, where the music was muffled. The end result—her purse was still gone, and she needed to call the bank and credit card companies.

By the time they'd finished up their report, Sabrina had to claim Ryan's arm for stability.

"Let's get you out of here," Ryan said, his arm wrapping around her waist.

"Please," she agreed. "Before I embarrass myself by getting sick would be the preference." She laughed, but it sounded more like a moan. "So much for romance, eh?"

"There's plenty of time for romance later," he assured her.

They said goodnight to their friends, Jennifer being

especially supportive and asking her to call her if she needed any help.

Thirty minutes later, Sabrina was on Ryan's cell phone talking to one of her credit-card companies when they pulled out of a fast food drive-through. Ryan had insisted she had to try to eat. But the scent of sausage and eggs engulfed her with a new wave of nausea.

"I can't eat anything right now," she moaned, hanging up to dial another number.

"Tomorrow you'll feel ten times worse, if you don't," he insisted.

"It's tonight I'm worried about," she said quickly.

"Worry is my job, remember?"

"Since your version of worry is not to worry," she said. "I'll carry the torch until I pass out. Then it's all yours."

"How soon is that going to be?"

She pressed her hand to her stomach. "Not soon enough, considering I should finish these calls."

His hand stroked her hair. "Rest," he said. "I'll wake you up when we get there."

Rest. Yes. She needed to rest. With her lashes heavy, stomach trembling and head pounding, sleep promised painless oblivion. Sabrina let the cell phone drop from her hand and curled her fingers under her cheek. Ryan's hand continued to lightly caress her head, soothing, comforting. And as she succumbed to the darkness—comfortable enough to simply allow Ryan to take care of her—she was pretty sure that meant something. Something important. Something she needed to remember tomorrow.

THE MINUTE RYAN LIFTED Sabrina out of the truck into his arms, she curled into him, sound asleep. Trusting. Protectiveness rose inside him, a feeling he was beginning to feel was synonymous with Sabrina. She played tough, pretended she could take care of herself. But he understood now what she'd meant when she'd said he left when she needed him. Sabrina had no one she could just be with, no one she didn't have to act tough around. And Ryan had made a decision tonight. He wanted to be that person, despite the risk of her using him to find herself and then taking off. He was all about risk and reward, and he wasn't going to turn away from that formula with Sabrina.

He'd already lodged open the hotel door, so a kick gave him entry, and he carried her inside. Carefully balancing Sabrina, he shut them safely inside the simple, no-frills room. There was a bed, a small kitchen and a bathroom, and not much more.

Settling Sabrina on the bed, he expected her to wake up any minute. She didn't move, completely knocked out. He tugged her high-heeled boots off one at a time and was about to tackle her jeans when she abruptly moaned and sat straight up. Wildly, she looked around trying to get her bearings before swallowing hard and half moaning, "Bathroom. I need a bathroom."

Ryan pointed to the open door, and she scooted off

the bed with newfound energy born of obvious desperation. Concerned, he followed, finding her hunched over the toilet, her hair draped over her face. Ryan sat down on the edge of the tub and lifted her hair, whispering comforting words as she fought the nausea.

After one particularly bad episode, she whispered, "I'm sorry." Slowly, she leaned back on her heels. "I'm so sorry for all of this, Ryan. This really wasn't how I would have liked this night to end up."

"Happens to the best of us," he assured her.

She leaned back on her heels again. "I must look horrible. Not exactly the way to make an impression."

"You had me at the mud mask," he teased.

She groaned at that. "Don't remind me." She tried to stand and wobbled.

Ryan quickly helped her. "Let's get you to bed."

"I have to shower," she said. "I feel disgusting."

"Maybe you should wait until morning," he said, wishing he had a real tub.

"I'll be okay," she said. "Really."

Skeptically, he agreed and turned the water on for her. She seemed steady enough to undress on her own. "I'll get you one of my shirts." He grabbed a towel off the rack. "The hotel's towels suck, but they get the job done." He closed the toilet seat and set one on the edge so she could reach it easily. "And don't even think about getting shy on me. I'm leaving the door open. I want to be able to hear you if you call me."

He didn't give her time to argue, exited to allow her to undress, returning once he was sure she was in the shower to leave her one of his Army T-shirts. He had no idea why, but he really wanted to see her in that shirt.

Pausing in the doorway, Ryan went completely, utterly still; the sight of Sabrina's naked silhouette against the shower curtain was so damn erotic, he had to swallow a groan. His hand went to the doorjamb. He was the one who suddenly was in need of steadying, his body raging with awareness, his cock expanding against his zipper. *Down, boy,* he silently ordered. Now was not the time.

He forced himself to set the shirt down, to walk out of the room. By the time the shower turned off, Ryan had grabbed some soda from the machine outside and changed into army sweats and a T-shirt to match Sabrina's. He intended to sleep in the sweats to ensure he kept his raging body in check until she was well.

He was in the kitchen filling a glass with ice when Sabrina appeared in the doorway, looking a bit tentative in his green shirt with *Army* stamped across it, her hair damp around her shoulders. Her nipples puckered against the thin material. Oh, yeah. He would never look at that shirt the same way again.

He held up the glass. "Soda?"

"Oh, yes, please," she said, closing the small space between them and drinking.

"Not too fast," he said, reaching for the glass. "You'll make yourself sick again."

"You're right," she said, eyeing the room. "Bed. Yes. That's what I need." She headed in that direction, no hesitation about climbing under the covers. "I hate the idea of wearing those clothes again tomorrow," she said, her eyes fluttering, lashes lowering.

Ryan sucked in a breath at the sight of her in his bed, adrenaline rushing over him. Images of all the ways he'd have his wicked way with her played in his head. He forced himself to slowly exhale and then inhale again. Willing his body to calm.

He forced his gaze from Sabrina, looked around the room, the barren, dismal room that wasn't much to see at all. A room meant to be temporary, but then temporary was comfortable, temporary was what he knew. Temporary housing, short-term missions and short-term women.

The only thing he'd ever believed was permanent in his life had been the Army. They'd been his family. The discovery he'd made had been a hard blow. Even now, he couldn't think about the betrayal that had led to his departure without his blood boiling.

Ryan's gaze flickered to where Sabrina lay peacefully sleeping in his bed, the sight of her calming the rise of turbulence inside him. His woman. The thought swelled inside him and expanded with a rush of possessive intensity that he'd never felt in his life.

The idea of Sabrina in his life, in his home, both enticed him and scared him. He was a fool for thinking like that. This wasn't even his bed or his home. It was a damn hotel. The same old temporary living arrangement called his life. And Sabrina would be the same old temporary relationship, too. He couldn't let himself forget that, couldn't let himself, or her, be convinced that this was more.

He'd been burned that way in his youth, thinking he was where he was supposed to be, with whom he was supposed to be. The only difference with Sabrina was, instead of him being the one making a short stop, it was her. Because, unlike him, she *had* a home—and that home was in New York. Ryan wasn't going to forget that. Which meant he'd better shake himself back to reality. Enjoy her as he did everything in life. Like it wasn't going to last. Because it never did.

14

SABRINA'S LASHES FLUTTERED OPEN, sunlight stroking her senses as readily as did the scent of something sweet and vanilla-scented cooking nearby. She lay there, snuggled in the blankets, her back to thc kitchen, then cringing when the events of the night before crept into disturbing clarity. Oh, good grief, she'd made a fool of herself. She squeezed her eyes shut at the memory of hanging over the toilet while Ryan held her hair out of her face. *Way to turn a guy on, Sabrina,* she chided herself silently. She didn't even want to imagine what she must look like right about now. If it compared to the taste in her mouth, it was pretty horrendous. But she'd made her mess, as her father would say, now she had to clean it up. Besides, her stomach was, remarkably, grumbling with demand.

Sabrina sat up, bringing Ryan into view, where he slaved over a stove. He seemed to sense her attention and turned to her.

"Morning," he said. His hair was damp, his face

clean-shaven, more handsome than rugged this morning. She swallowed against the dryness in her throat.

"Morning." Suddenly, she was aware that she was not only wearing his shirt, she was in "the bed," the only bed in the place.

"How do you feel?"

She considered the question. "Surprisingly okay. And hungry. What are you cooking that smells so good?"

"Pancakes," he said, turning the pan off. "I figured they'd be easier on your stomach than eggs or bacon." He set two plates on the bar dividing the tiny kitchen from the rest of the room. A stool sat on either side. "You up to joining me or you want me to bring it to you?"

"I can come there," she said, embarrassed at how he'd been waiting on her. "You've done enough." She scooted to the edge of the bed and hesitated. "Oh, man. It tastes like something died in my mouth. Yuk. I don't suppose you have an extra toothbrush?"

"You're in luck," he said. "Bought a new one I haven't opened. Under the bathroom sink."

"Oh, good," she said, tiptoeing toward the bathroom, ever aware she wore only his shirt. "Thank you."

She quickly disappeared into the bathroom and shut the door. The instant she saw herself in the mirror, she about died. Her face was pale, except for the beautiful dark smudges of mascara under her eyes. Her hair was a wild nest that looked like a bird might hatch from the top. She remembered now that she'd washed her hair and not dried it. Note to self—bad idea.

She opened the cabinet and found the toothbrush.

Then, a hairbrush. She sudsed up her face with some men's brand of face soap and used moisturizer. It smelled liked Ryan, woodsy and masculine. The shirt didn't. Next time, she wanted to wear one he'd worn first. Next time. Next time?

She grabbed the door and pulled it open, unable to bear the idea of not knowing what had happened between them. Ryan paused, about to fill two glasses with orange juice, giving her that silent, arched-brow look she'd become accustomed to.

"I don't remember going to bed," she said, her voice lifting more than she meant it to. "Did we…you know… sleep together?"

Leaning on the counter, he studied her. "Yes. We slept together."

Her heart jumped wildly in her chest. They'd slept together, and she didn't remember. How could this be? How could she forget having sex with Ryan?!

"As in, slept, Sabrina," Ryan said, chuckling. "Just sleep. Nothing else."

Relief washed over her before his little trick hit home. She admonished. "That was just plain evil. You know what you made me think."

His gaze swept her body, appreciation in his eyes. "Evil is you in that shirt and me having to go to work. Come eat. Your food is getting cold. Caleb's picking me up in half an hour. I'll leave you my truck and my phone. Use my truck for whatever."

She hurried to the bar stool and sat down across from him. "I can't take your truck," she said. "Or your phone.

What if you need them? And what if I get stopped? I have no license."

"Police report is in the truck," he said. "That and a smile should keep you out of trouble. I'll be working anyway. You might as well put them to use." He claimed the seat across from her and filled the two coffee cups. "And I don't want you to go back to your place until I can change the locks. You'll need to get another key from whomever you rent from, though. If you can pick me up at work, we can go by and pick up your car—the dealership can get you a key—and then head to your place to change the locks."

"Ryan," she argued. "I can't ask you to do all of this."

"You don't have to ask," he said. "That's what friends are for."

"Friends," she said uncomfortably. Had last night scared him away from more? "Is that what we are?"

"Yeah," he said. "We're friends." He gave her a crooked smiled. "Friends with benefits. And don't you forget it."

"I won't forget, if you don't," she said tentatively, thinking of the turbulence between them yet to be fully resolved.

His eyes twinkled. "You can remind me tonight."

Tonight. She smiled at that; the idea of actually sleeping with Ryan and remembering it was a good one. They ate then, the news playing in the background. Sabrina shocked herself by putting down four pancakes, orange juice and coffee. Ryan managed double that and said he was still hungry.

They were almost finished when a news story caught her ear. Sabrina grabbed the remote sitting on the bar between them and turned up the volume as the newscaster reported, "Sources near the mayor say the wife of the deceased soldier visited his office after hours, a week before the soldier died. The mayor calls the claim absolutely false, and meant to stir headlines."

She should have known the story would get out before she had time to finish investigating. Frank was going to be furious. "That's the soldier I wrote that article about," she told Ryan, "the one I thought might be suffering from post-traumatic stress disorder—"

"Wait," Ryan said. "*You* wrote that article?"

"Oh, ah, yeah," she said. "My boss forced me to cover the story, and I agreed as long as no one, not even the staff at the paper, knew who'd penned it. He had a tip that there was a cover-up going on, but I haven't found anything to support that. But this…this is big. Why would that soldier's wife visit the mayor?"

"What happened to wanting out of politics? Starting a new life?"

"You're right," she said. "Absolutely right. I guess carracing just isn't overly exciting. I need to find something that is. Not that I'm complaining. It's a doorway to the next venue, when I figure out what that is, and I am so very grateful for that." The subject of her past jogged her memory, reminding her about what Ryan had said in the bar. "Ryan. About that night at my apartment…"

"It's the past," he said quickly, too quickly, but gently. Without any hint of tension. "Leave it there. Isn't that what we were just talking about? Moving on?"

"Yes," she agreed. "But I need you to know I wanted you because of you. Because of what you make me feel."

His eyes glinted with interest. "Which is what?"

She thought about the stairwell, the mud mask, him holding her hair while she threw up. "Like I can be me and you won't judge me. I worry enough about things like last night getting into the news. Or used against my father. But you, Ryan…you just let me be me, even when that me isn't so spectacular."

Seconds ticked by, his expression indecipherable, before he said, "I'm glad." He eyed the watch on his arm, a Swiss Army brand which looked masculine and right on him. He picked up the plates and turned to the sink. "Caleb's going to be here in ten minutes. I need to get moving."

Sabrina stared at his back, trying to figure out what she'd said wrong, because it was obvious she had.

She scooted off the chair and walked to the tiny kitchen to stand next to him. "I'll wash the dishes," she offered. "You cooked."

He turned to her and neither of them spoke, a hint of tension crackling around them. "Sabrina," he said.

"Yes?" she asked, hanging on his words, hoping to understand what had shifted his mood.

But he said nothing, seeming to change his mind. He reached for her. The kiss that followed was a silky caress of tongue against tongue, full of dark emotion and hunger. She raised up on her toes, arched into him. When finally it was over, she panted with need. His hands rested on her waist, teasing her with where else they might go.

"Thank you on the dishes," he said.

"If that kiss was my thank-you," she whispered, "I'll make a habit of doing your dishes."

"I can think of better things than dishes to barter with," he assured her. "I'll demonstrate tonight." He released her, and she ached to pull him back to her.

"Here are my keys," he said, fishing them from his pocket. "And my cell." He opened a drawer and scribbled a number. "That's the Hotzone. Call me there if you need me. I'm off at four."

After he was gone, she sat on the end of his bed eyeing the tiny hotel room. Wondering why he had chosen to stay here instead of renting an apartment for six months to a year. She vowed to help him find his perfect home, the way he was helping her find herself.

Inhaling, she drew in the delicious scent of his cologne and fell back on his bed. He was nothing like the men of her past. Change was good. It was really good.

"SINCE I ALMOST got my ass beat for dancing with this chick," Caleb said, on the drive from the hotel to the Hotzone, "I'm assuming it's pretty serious."

Ryan scowled at Caleb from the passenger's seat. "I didn't almost beat your ass."

"You acted like you were about to rip my head off

my shoulders," he said. "And you know, it's cool an' all. You didn't, which, in the end, is what counts. So what's the story?"

"It's a good time," Ryan said. "Nothing more."

"Not buying that one. You gave her your truck, your cell phone and you left her alone in your house."

"It's a hotel room," Ryan stated. "I hardly think that means anything."

Caleb pulled to a stop at a red light and gave Ryan a keen inspection. "Ryan, after the way you behaved last night, you really expect me to believe this chick is riding around in your truck while you're just taking her for a ride?"

Ryan clamped a hand over his jaw a moment, and considered denial, which turned into a confession. "It's more like she's taking me for a ride."

"She seems pretty into you, man," Caleb observed.

"Of course she is," Ryan said. "She ran to Texas to find herself an adventure, and she's decided that's me. I'm the guy who helps her find herself, so someone else gets the prize."

"Not a bad thing," Caleb said. "Unless you want the prize. Then it sucks."

"Yeah," Ryan agreed. "Then it sucks."

15

STILL AT RYAN'S HOTEL, Sabrina had completed her calls, her arrangements made—but she had one major problem. With no clothes, no makeup, no money and no identification to prove she was who she said she was, she had no choice but to swing by her place. She was nervous about an intruder, but the property manager, a sweet woman in her fifties named Nelda, met Sabrina at the door.

"I can't believe your purse was stolen," Nelda exclaimed. "My goodness, honey, you look like you've been put through the wringer. Were you mugged?"

Nelda—who Sabrina knew to be one of the top Realtors in the city—was dressed in jeans and Western shirt. Casual, kind and concerned.

"No, no," she said. "I was silly enough to leave my purse unattended. I know better. Thankfully, a friend let me stay the night, but I am so looking forward to my own clothes."

"Well, I'm just glad you're safe," Nelda said, touching

Sabrina's arm. "And, honey, we all make mistakes. Don't be too hard on yourself."

The sincerity in the woman amazed Sabrina. The New York version of Nelda would have worn a classic Ann Taylor pantsuit, her idea of casual Saturday, and she would have given Sabrina a scornful eye for Ryan's T-shirt tied at her waist, yesterday's well-worn jeans, and her hair puffed up like a poodle.

"I'll wait out here while you get your things," Nelda said. "It's terrifying to think of someone with your ID and address having your keys. Are you sure you don't want me to change the locks for you? I can get a locksmith in. Of course, it's very expensive on the weekend. I'd hate for you to incur that cost."

"I have a friend who said he can handle it for me tonight," she assured Nelda. *Plus it's a good way to ensure Ryan comes over tonight,* she added silently. "I'll give you the new key on Monday." Sabrina grabbed the doorknob. "Okay, so if I scream, call the police."

"Oh, don't say things like that," Nelda admonished. "Maybe we should have someone check out the place first."

"No," Sabrina said. "It's fine. I'll be in and out in a snap."

Despite her bravado, Sabrina rushed into her apartment, her heart thundering in her chest. She darted down the hall, and quickly searched under her bed and in the closets. The idea of changing here as she'd planned suddenly seemed scary, and she didn't want Nelda to have to wait. She grabbed a bag and started tossing things inside, including her passport for ID, and her computer. Then she rushed down the hall, said her quick goodbyes to Nelda, and headed to the parking lot. She'd swing by the hotel and change, and then get moving on her errands.

As soon as she arrived back at the hotel, she rushed into the bathroom and stripped down to nothing, eager to change and get to the bank before they closed. She had no credit card, no ATM card, no cash, no way to pay for the new key at the car dealership, and tomorrow was Sunday—no banks would be open. But dang it, she was going to see Ryan in a few hours. She needed to wash her hair and look presentable. She peeked out of the bathroom and eyed the clock. Noon. She still had time.

Ten minutes later, with a tiny towel wrapped around her, she applied makeup and turned on the dryer attached to the wall. The minute it turned off, she heard the cell phone on the last ring of a call. It had to be for Ryan. It was his phone, and he would be the only one who might call her, but he was probably jumping out of a plane right now. Sabrina smoothed her hair, satisfied she was all set. Feeling better, she headed to the main room to get dressed.

She'd just dropped her towel when a knock sounded on the door. "Sabrina, it's Ryan."

She reached for the towel, wrapped it around herself. "I thought you were working."

"A large group cancelled," he said. "I took a cab. I tried to call. Are you going to let me in?"

Frantically she dug in her bag for clothes, frustrated when she couldn't get to them. "Ah, Sabrina?" Ryan said. "Any time now."

She looked down at her towel. Considered her options. He'd turned her down once. Did she dare risk that again? Well. If he did, at least she wouldn't have any regrets, beyond her own embarrassment. She was done with regrets.

Sabrina walked over to the door and flipped the latch, then popped the handle. She stayed behind the door and let him enter the room. When the door shut behind him, she was exposed.

She stepped forward and did something she'd never done with another man—took a huge risk, exposing herself fully both emotionally and, yes, physically.

Sabrina dropped her towel. "Welcome home, honey."

RYAN FROZE, AFRAID IF HE MOVED he'd wake up, because he must be dreaming. Sabrina, gloriously naked, greeting him at the door. It was too good to be true. If this wasn't something that could make anyplace home, he didn't know what would. Hunger clawed at him, instant and demanding, his gaze sweeping over Sabrina's amazing, sexy body, her dark hair caressing creamy shoulders, hair he fully intended to see on his stomach, his chest. And her breasts—high, full, with plump, pink nipples that he wanted in his mouth.

"Ryan," Sabrina pleaded. "Please say or do something or I am going to die of mortification."

His gaze jerked to hers. "Mortification?" He closed the distance between them and pulled her to the bed where he sat down, holding her between his legs. "Sweetheart." His hand flattened on her belly. "You are absolutely beautiful. I was just trying to figure out if this is a dream." His hands traveled up her waist, over her breasts. He pressed them together and thumbed her nipples, then licked. One nipple, then the other. "And enjoying the view."

"Last time—"

He took her down on the mattress, on her back, him beside her, on his side. His hand settling again on her stomach—there was something so damn sexy about her stomach. "Last time I was so worried about taking advantage of you being upset, I didn't see the big picture. That you were reaching out to me in a moment of need. I'm sorry."

She rolled to her side, her hand to his cheek, and kissed him. "I wanted you, Ryan. All my father's note did was remind me I'd given up too much of my life, that I'd missed out on things I didn't want to miss. Like you. You are, without exception, the best thing that has happened to me in a very long time."

Ryan inhaled those words as a dying man would his last breath, his lips lingering over hers, their breaths weaving together as one. Once again he found himself frozen, afraid to move for fear this would be a dream. He was falling for this woman, probably already had. Falling in love, and he could do nothing in that moment but embrace the absoluteness as it came to him. She didn't want to miss out on him. Well, he didn't want to miss out on her either. And for now, in this room, she was his. And he wanted everything, all of her. Every last moan, every bit of emotion and passion.

"Ryan," she said, pulling back, apparently mistaking his silence as negative. "I didn't mean to say the wrong thing. I mean, I know I'm probably not the type of woman you—"

He rolled her to her back, slid between her legs. "The only type I have is you. You totally do it for me, Sabrina. In every possible way."

"I do?"

"Oh, yeah, sweetheart," he promised. "You do. And I'm going to show you just how much."

SABRINA'S INSECURITY, her fear, was gone. Everything about Ryan's reaction, his words, the hunger radiating from him, filled her with confidence, ignited her need for him.

Ryan brushed his lips over hers, as if to seal his promise, a soft whisper brushed with such intense sensuality that goose bumps slid along her skin. "No barriers this time," he vowed.

She had no idea what that meant, but it sounded good, sounded really good. That was, until he pulled back. She reached for him, desperate to bring him back, to feel his weight on her, to feel him touch her and kiss her.

But he was standing at the end of the bed, undressing, yanking his shirt over his head. Sabrina lifted herself to her elbows, forgetting any nerves over her own nudity. It was midday, and sunlight beamed through the thin hotel curtains, highlighting Ryan's full form, leaving nothing to her imagination. And he was perfect. The width of his shoulders, the exact right amount of light-brown hair sprinkled across his impressive chest. Dark, flat nipples. She swallowed hard as she discovered a thin line of hair that trailed down his spectacular abdominals and disappeared beneath his jeans. Which he unsnapped.

"We should talk about birth control," he said.

Her gaze jerked upward. "Birth control?" she asked, not quite registering the question. That line of hair was just so intriguing.

"Yeah," he said. "Let's do 'the talk' and get it out of the way."

"The talk." Laughter bubbled from her lips, with surprising ease, considering this was her first time to be naked with Ryan—well, sort of, there was the partial nudity in the stairwell. But normally she'd be nervous, thinking about what he was thinking. But the heat in his eyes, the stark hunger in his face, said more than words. Continuing, she said playfully, "Well, let's see. I'm on the pill, but a good senator's daughter would still demand a condom. Got one?"

He reached to a drawer behind him and tossed a row of condom packages to the bed. "Never had sex without one. The women in my life haven't exactly stayed around long."

She snatched the six-pack of condoms from the bed. "Glad you're prepared." Was she one of the here-today, gone-tomorrow women of his life? Another conquest. Another goodbye.

"Don't go reading into that," he said, as if he was the one reading *her* mind. "I'm not bed-hopping. I haven't, not for a good long while. I was on a mission for six months right before I got out of the Army. You?"

The last man in her bed had been a corporate attorney she'd thought wanted her, wining and dining her, sending her flowers. But in bed, he'd been hard and fast, and insensitive to her needs. Satisfaction for him. None for her. She'd given him three tries, all of which had left her feeling used and abused. When she'd broken up with him, he'd told her she was boring in bed, and that he'd tolerated her for her father's business.

"A year," she said, a bit more somber now. Was she boring in bed? Had she been the problem?

"I bought them the night I met you," Ryan said, drawing her into the moment, the look in his eyes, the understanding that seemed to reach beyond words. He made her feel sexy, made her feel confident.

She shoved away the past and reveled in the moment, in Ryan. "A bit presumptuous, don't you think?" she asked, casting him in a haunting look.

"A soldier is both prepared and thorough," he amended, hungrily inspecting her body, his gaze lingering on her nipples. "Damn, you're beautiful, woman." The words seemed to set off an urgency within him.

In one swift move, his jeans and boxers were gone. A wave of overwhelming, almost primal need washed over her as she found the answer to where that trail of hair ended. He was all sinewy muscle, defined, powerful. Aroused. His erection impressively long and hard.

Before she knew his intention, his knees hit the mattress, and he turned her to her stomach. He spread her legs and slipped between, his body warm over hers, his lips near her ear.

"Thorough, remember," he whispered. "I want to know all of you, Sabrina. Every last inch."

It was complete submission. It was handing him control. And it was having control. Because it was her decision. One so much more meaningful than that one moment at the edge of a plane when the decision to jump took place. It was intimate. It was personal. It was trust.

He brushed her hair from her neck and nibbled. Spread her arms out and covered them with his own, and pressed his lips between her shoulder blades. His cock settled between her legs, slid into the wet heat, taunting her with how easily it would be for him to slip inside her.

His hands caressed a path down her arms until they slipped around her, cupping her breasts. She moaned and bit her lip. He tugged gently on her nipples, pressed his hips more fully between her thighs. Her backside lifted, as desperation tore through her.

"Ryan," she whispered. "Oh..." She lost the words as he moved, leaving her thighs aching. His mouth traveled down her spine, hands down her ribcage, over her hips, her backside. Kissing a path that was rapidly becoming more tempting, more intimate. Sabrina could feel herself losing touch with reality, her body quivering with every touch, every taste.

By the time his fingers slid between her legs, she cried out, gasping on a plea. "Ryan. Please."

He slid up her body, hard muscle encasing her everywhere, the thick ridge of his shaft teasing her thighs. Yes. That's what she wanted. "Please what?" he asked, his cheek next to hers.

"You know what I want," she whispered. "You."

"Me how?"

For only a flash of a second, she hesitated, not used to being uninhibited with a man. But it was a second and gone. "Inside me. I want to feel you inside me."

"And you will," he promised. "Soon."

He lifted his body off hers, rolled to his side, and Sabrina took advantage, not giving him the chance to claim control again. She'd given it. Now she wanted to take it. It was her turn to drive him crazy.

Sabrina straddled Ryan, positioning the hard length of his erection behind her, pressing temptingly against her backside. "My turn," she declared, driven by how much this man turned her on—everything about him, including the wicked gleam in his eye right now.

"And if I say no?" he challenged.

She leaned down, the crisp hair of his chest teasing her nipples. "Don't you want to please me?"

His hands ran up her back, the air crackling with instant heat. "You know I do."

She did; she knew. That was what made it so easy to be free with him. "Then *do* what I say."

He nipped her bottom lip and smiled. "I thought you weren't a control freak?"

"Sometimes control has its perks."

His hand slid into her hair. "Sometimes giving away control has its perks." He dragged her mouth to his, a bit rough, a lot wild. His tongue pressed into her mouth, a deep, drugging invasion that Sabrina felt in every nerve ending of her body. Her thighs hugged his waist, wet heat draped across his lower stomach. It would be so easy to lift her body and take him inside her. So good to take him inside her. She fought the urge. There was so much she wanted to do to him first. So much.

He broke the kiss long enough to nip and nibble her lip, his hand at the back of her neck, holding her captive until he claimed another drugging kiss, taking her further into an alternate reality where only pleasure existed. He reached between them, tugging at her nipples, tweaking with enough pressure that it hurt, but, oh, so good.

He turned his face to her hair and then nuzzled her cheek. "You smell gorgeous. Like honeysuckle." His hands covered her breasts, held them, caressed them.

"My shampoo," she whispered absently, the press of his shaft against her back reminding her of her agenda. How she wanted to slide down his body and take his cock in her mouth. To show him the kind of pleasure he had shown her.

Desperate to make it happen, she pressed away from him, sitting up. "And stop it. Control is not yours right now."

"Sweetheart," he said, his voice low, rough. "I couldn't agree more. I am totally at your mercy, unable to stop touching you." He reached for her.

She captured his hands with hers, twined her fingers with his. "Behave, Ryan Walker."

His gaze brushed her nipples. "Let me lick one."

"I said behave."

"Let me lick one and I will."

"Stop," she ordered.

An evil smile touched those equally evil lips capable of amazing things. "You know you want me to."

"No," she lied. "I don't." Yes. She did. Her nipples were perhaps the most erogenous places on her body. Along with the back of her neck, which he'd effortlessly located quite effectively.

"Let me lick one and I'll behave."

Tempting. "You promise?"

"You have my word."

His word. She believed him more the last time he'd offered it. He was in naughty mode. Wickedly naughty and she loved it. "Fine." Holding on to his hands, she leaned forward, dangling her nipple excruciatingly close to his mouth before saying, "Remember your promise."

Hunger flitted across his face. "I remember."

She leaned into him, and he did more than lick. He suckled her nipple into his mouth. Sabrina moaned with the sensation, waves of it washing over her and into her. Her back arched into him, thrusting her breasts higher. Her grip on his hand weakened, forgotten. He licked and suckled and nipped. His teeth rough, his tongue gentle. Her hips were moving; she couldn't help it. She needed him. She needed and needed.

"It's time to let me inside, Sabrina," he said, his hand twining into her hair and dragging her mouth to his. Masterfully, he both kissed her and lifted her hips, shifting her body until he pressed the head of his shaft past her swollen, aching flesh.

Sabrina held her breath as he slipped all the way inside her. "Oh," she moaned as she felt him fill her, expand within her.

His fingers brushed through her hair. "*Oh* is right," he breathed into her mouth, briefly tasting her.

"You're very...hard," she whispered. And big.

He laughed. "That's the idea, isn't it?"

Smiling, she said, "Yeah, but you are exceptionally—" He thrust into her, pressing her hips against his.

"Hard," he said, finishing her sentence.

"Yes."

"That's because you really turn me on, Sabrina," he said, his hands going to her face, bringing her gaze to his. "You...like no other woman."

It was a confession that took her by surprise. Shook her to the core. Excited her. Frightened her. This man was inside her in more ways than the physical. She opened her mouth to confess as much, but her throat constricted. He was so much more than sex. He could hurt her. What if he hurt her?

"Prove it," she finally said. "Prove it now."

For just an instant a shadow flickered across his face. Disappointment perhaps. Or not. Perhaps she'd imagined it because almost instantly a primal look full of pure male intent filled his expression.

He took her mouth then, took it with a savageness she'd not felt from him until now. His shaft seemed to thicken further, pulsing inside her. She'd called him wild, but now she, too, was wild. They began to move together, hips pumping and grinding. Bodies pressed close, as if that would take him deeper. As if that would tear down what little separated them. Until the rage of need slowed to a sultry, sensual dance. Until the wild tasting of tongues became a soft musical caress. Until their eyes met and spoke for them.

There was something happening between them, something neither controlled any more than they did their burn to get closer. One last wild rush overcame them, a frenzied thrusting and pumping, that took Sabrina to the edge of shattering where she clung for dear life, wanting this to last, wanting…wanting. Until she shattered, burying her head in his neck, and gasping a moment before the spasms clamped down on his shaft, her body taking what it had wanted from the moment she first met him. He tumbled right after her, shuddered with a hard lift of his hips as he cupped her backside and buried himself far and deep.

SABRINA LAY ON TOP of Ryan, a limp noodle of satisfaction, when suddenly it hit her. "The bank!" she yelped, scrambling to the edge of the bed. "I have to get to the bank." She eyed the clock. "Thirty minutes. I'm never going to make it! I have no ID, no money, no way to pay for my car keys." She scrambled for her bag and clothes.

"I thought you went earlier," Ryan said, already standing and putting on his pants.

"No, I—" Something scraped her back, and she reached over her shoulder. "Ouch! What is that."

Ryan snatched whatever it was off her back and held it up. The condoms. "I think I'm the one who is supposed to wear them, not you."

The condoms they hadn't used were not her biggest problem right now. It was money. "Hurry," she ordered. "Get dressed."

His gaze caught on the jeans she pulled from her bag. "Where did that come from? Wait. Your shampoo. Your hair smelled like honeysuckle. You went to your apartment. Sabrina, damn it, what were you thinking?"

"That I had to have my passport to prove to the bank I'm me." Damn. Her shirt must be in the bathroom. She turned toward it.

Ryan shackled her arm, halting her movement. "Are you nuts? What if someone was watching you at the club? What if they had targeted you?"

"The property manager came with me," she said. "Or rather she waited in the hall ready to call for help."

"Oh, that was safe," he chided shortly. "Damn it. You should have called me."

"Don't curse at me, Ryan Walker."

"Don't put yourself in danger, and I won't."

"You aren't my protector."

"Yeah, well, maybe I should be."

She gaped. "What the heck does that mean?"

"It means I care about you. And if you stand there naked much longer, yelling at me, I'm going to throw you on the bed and show you how much."

Sabrina snatched the towel from the floor and wrapped it around herself. Though the idea that he couldn't resist her wore away at her frustration.

Ryan sat down on the edge of the bed. "Look. Sabrina. I'm sorry. Whatever this is that's going on between us, it makes me protective. I've seen some nasty things. Imagining the motives behind stealing your purse isn't hard for me."

Sabrina blinked at both the content of his confession and the delivery, glimpsing the tiniest bit of vulnerability and uncertainty behind his words. As if he wasn't sure how she would respond. He touched her, this big, confident, sexy man with a softer side that even an argument couldn't hide.

Closing the distance between them, she stopped in front of him, and gently touched his cheek. "No one has ever protected me before. Not me. Just my reputation. I like it."

Surprise flickered in his face. "You do?"

She nodded. "Yes. Very much." A slow smile slid to her lips. "But you think you can tame just a little bit of the tough-guy, demanding thing?"

He drew her hand to his mouth. "Depends. Can I still be tough-guy and demanding in bed?"

Instant sexual energy charged the room. "Sometimes," she negotiated.

"Now?"

She glanced at the clock. No way was she making it to the bank. And she wasn't sure she'd care if she could. "Now," she agreed and dropped her towel in the name of seduction for the second time in one day.

16

DESPITE A WHIRLWIND of errands, and more than their share of challenges along the way, Ryan had enjoyed the hell out of spending the rest of Saturday with Sabrina. It was near eight that night when they finally stepped into the elevator of her building, several bags in hand, including a lock kit, a gourmet heat-and-eat pizza—since they hadn't had time to eat—and her new cell phone in need of charging.

"I still can't believe my car was impounded," Sabrina murmured, shaking her head. Her car had been one of their more complicated challenges. "The manager at the bar promised us that wouldn't happen when my purse was stolen. I even called this morning, and they said it was there." Animated, she turned to him. "And after you paid for my key. I feel horrible about that."

"You still need the key," he reminded her. "And I can drive you out to the lot to get your car Monday morning when the tow company reopens," he offered.

"I don't want you to miss more work than you have," she argued. "You missed today."

"Business was slow," Ryan said. "Besides, I worked seven days a week for over a month getting ready for the Hotzones first Army training camp. I'm due a few hours here or there."

The elevator dinged and opened on her floor. "You're sure?"

"Positive," he said as they exited into her hallway. "And for selfish reasons. I'd like to take you out dancing again sometime. That means erasing the bad memories as soon as possible."

"I don't even want to think about how I was carrying on at that bar," she grimaced. "If I'd been in New York, someone would have snapped a picture and held it for ransom for sure."

He snagged her hand and pulled her close. "But you're not in New York. You're in Texas. With me."

She smiled. "And I'm liking being in Texas." She kissed him. "With you. But please. Stop me at one margarita next time."

"You have my word."

Her smile widened to a grin. "Yes. I have your word." She started to turn.

He didn't let her get away, tugging on her hand. "And that makes you smile, why?"

She glanced over her shoulder, pulling him forward. "Because you always say that, and I know you mean it. I like it." She stopped abruptly, and Ryan almost ran into her.

"Easy there, sweetheart," he warned and then frowned, noting the box in front of her door.

"Your father again?" he asked, feeling his gut tighten.

"I don't know," she said. "I haven't been taking his calls. Or my mother's, for that matter. So maybe. Every time I talk to them they tell me all the reasons why I should go back to New York. Our conversations always end badly." She approached the door and Ryan followed, taking the bag she had in her hand and shuffling it to the hand where he held the other two.

He watched her bend down and study the package, his nerves prickling with discomfort. Today, he'd actually begun to think Sabrina might really want to stay here, to make a life here. Maybe with him. But there was one man Ryan knew he couldn't compete with—her father.

"Weird," she said. "There isn't a return address or any postage."

"Put it down," Ryan ordered with such force that Sabrina dropped the box immediately.

"Why? What?" She held her hand to her chest. "You scared the heck out of me."

Ryan set the bags down. "Back away and let me check it out." He waited for her compliance and then squatted by the box. Bent his head and listened for any odd sound and then did a visual inspection.

Standing up, he turned to Sabrina. "Hand me your keys."

"Ryan, what is going on?" she asked.

His fingers brushed her jaw. "I'm having one of those protective moments that you both love and hate. Your purse was stolen. We have to be cautious. Stay out here. I'll open the package."

"Why?" she asked, alarm flushing her cheeks. "Do you think it's going to blow up or there's a dead animal inside, or something creepy like that?"

Ryan settled his hands on her face. "Sabrina, sweetheart. Just trust me, okay? Let me do this, and then we can make our pizza and enjoy it." He brushed his lips over hers. "And each other."

She hesitated but nodded. "Okay." He started to pull away, and she grabbed one of his hands. "Should we call the police?"

"I have far more training than anyone who would show up, I swear."

"Oh, right," she said. "But still..."

"I'll be careful," he promised. She was worried. About a box hurting him. How would she have been if she'd known him when he was gone for months, completely out of touch? "Stay right there until I call you."

Ryan had already assessed the telltale signs of an amateur at work: the way the box was taped. And it was a recycled box from a local food manufacturer, which meant the person wasn't worried about being traced. It also meant this package wasn't from Sabrina's parents.

First, Ryan unlocked her door and then cautiously picked up the package. "Be careful," Sabrina called.

Despite the disconcerting circumstances, Ryan smiled

as he entered the apartment and shut the door. He didn't stop until he reached Sabrina's kitchen, the opposite side of the living room, away from the windows and enclosed to absorb any blast, although he wasn't expecting one. The kitchen also put him a good distance from the door, this allowed him to respond to whatever was inside if necessary, without endangering Sabrina.

He set the box down, pulled out a chair and set his cell on it. Then he grabbed a knife from the kitchen block. He sliced the box open and backed up, then waited. Nothing. Next he flipped the lid open. Waited again. Nothing. Finally, he knocked it to its side. Sabrina's purse tumbled out. What the heck?

Using the knife, he investigated the easy-to-access items lying on the table. No note. Nothing but the purse. Nothing that he could see. For further investigation, Ryan grabbed a towel from the kitchen to avoid touching anything, dumped the contents of the purse on the table, and went through it. Lipstick, powder, keys. Wallet. He struggled with the towel, but managed to open the wallet and review the contents. Everything seemed to be inside. Driver's license. Credit cards. Even forty dollars in cash.

Ryan didn't like it one bit. Someone was messing with her. A stalker maybe? They should file a police report as soon as possible.

Hating that he had to scare Sabrina, Ryan did a quick check of the condo, and then headed to the hallway.

"Well?" Sabrina asked anxiously.

He grabbed their shopping bags from the ground and motioned her inside. "Let's go inside and talk."

The color drained from her face. "What does that mean?"

"Inside," he said again.

Ryan disposed of the bags by the door and led Sabrina to the table. "My purse!" she exclaimed excitedly and reached for it.

"Don't touch it," Ryan warned, "we need to have it fingerprinted."

"What? Why?"

"No note and everything is intact. Even the forty bucks in your wallet. I assume that's what you had in it?"

"Yes," she said. "Couldn't this be a nice person who didn't want a reward?"

"Maybe," he said. "I just don't like the way this feels, Sabrina. Better safe than sorry. Let's call the police and let them do a report. That way if this person who dropped it off becomes a problem, you have a record."

"Now you're really starting to freak me out," she said.

He wrapped her in his arms. "I don't mean to. But don't count on getting rid of me tonight. I'm not leaving you alone until we're sure about this."

She smiled, but it didn't reach her eyes. "One perk to being a damsel in distress," she said. "Having you around as my personal bodyguard."

Over an hour later, the police officer, a twenty-something kid still wet behind the ears, wrapped up his questions. "Is there anything else I should know? You're sure there have been no other indicators of threats?"

Ryan remembered Sabrina's answering machine in the kitchen. "You should check your messages before he leaves."

"No," Sabrina said quickly, running her hands down her hips and regrouping. "I mean, I cleared them while you guys were talking. There's nothing of concern there."

Even the young buck of a cop wasn't convinced. "You sure, ma'am?"

"Yes," she said. "Very sure. Thank you so much for coming out. I'm hoping this is a false alarm."

When the cop exited, Sabrina shut the door, locked it and turned to Ryan. He stood, arms crossed, waiting for her. "What was that about?"

"I just wanted him gone," she said. "I wanted this over with."

"What aren't you telling me, Sabrina?"

"Any messages are most likely from my parents. I'm really liking my private sanctuary called Texas. And though I cling to the hope my father won't run for the White House, albeit I'd never tell him that, I don't want to lose my privacy because this latest crazy installment of my life might make the news. It's sad, but true."

He understood. He understood, and he hated the truth of her words. She couldn't escape that part of her life, and he couldn't protect her from it, no matter how much he might try. He could only help her deal with it.

"We should listen to the messages," he said. "Or I

can give you some privacy to listen to them. Both home and cell phone."

A defeated sigh followed. "You might as well listen with me," she said, motioning him toward the kitchen. "If you're going to be in my life, you need to know what that means, good and bad. There's no better way than a good dose of my parents to give you the full picture."

There were ten messages. Ryan thought for sure they couldn't all be from her parents. They were. The final one played.

"Sabrina, this is your mother. I know you're alive and well because I read your feature on that car driver, which surprised me, of course, but that's another subject. You should be doing what you do well. Politics."

"Now that it serves Daddy's campaign," Sabrina mumbled.

The message continued, "We're worried. Please call us. Or I'm going to get on a plane and come there."

"Oh, crap," Sabrina said, leaning her elbows on the counter and dropping her head. "She means it. I have to call. I should check my cell phone and make sure her threats haven't become more urgent. I might have to make that call to her tonight."

"I'll change the locks while you check your cell," he suggested. "That pizza would taste really good right about now, as well."

"I'll pop it in," she agreed.

Ryan headed to the door, wondering what was really keeping Sabrina from calling her parents. Ten calls were a lot of calls. And sure, Ryan understood she was avoiding their nudge back into politics, but he had to wonder if there was more to her avoidance. Perhaps she knew that this nudge was all it would take to talk her into returning to New York.

SABRINA SAT DOWN at the dining-room table and stared at the mess that was her purse. While preferring to believe a good Samaritan had returned it, there was no question she was shaken. The idea of a stranger digging through her personal items, knowing her address—it was hard not to be unsettled. Having Ryan change her locks and stay close was comforting. And having him close, well… She was falling for him. She *had* fallen for him. For the first time in her life, she was pretty sure she was feeling love for this man. It was early in the relationship, she knew, but she'd dated men casually for months and never once had she even begun to think such a thing.

All the more reason why she didn't want to call home. Home. Was New York home? She stared out the window, at the Austin view she'd come to love. The city life emulating a small-town feel, with its casual attire, a downtown you could stroll without being mauled and such friendly people. And Ryan. Ryan was here.

Tension radiated up her spine as she grabbed her cell phone. It was dead. She snatched the bag by her chair, pulled out the charger she'd bought for the new phone she no longer needed, and plugged it into the wall. The instant the phone lit up, it rang. Frank. At least it wasn't her father.

Sabrina hit the answer button and was immediately greeted with, "What's going on, Cameron?"

Last-name usage. Never a good sign. She opened her mouth to speak.

He cut her off. "You don't know how to answer your phone or what? You're too good to work on the weekends? You're no diva here in Texas. You answer your phone."

Sabrina smiled. She couldn't help it. "This diva," she replied, "had her purse, car keys and cell phone stolen. Would you like a copy of the police report? Or maybe I should write a story about it."

"Actually—"

"No," she said sharply. "It was a joke, Frank."

"It would sell papers," he countered. "Don't offer if you aren't willing to pay up."

"I assume there was a reason I was scolded for not answering my phone?"

"You saw the story about that soldier," he demanded, rather than asked.

"I saw it."

"We should have had that story."

Sabrina ground her teeth. "Why didn't your political team get it?"

"I gave you this story," he quipped sharply. "*You,* Sabrina. And I sent you the names of people involved, details to follow up on, yet you let someone else get the real story. You gave me fluff."

"And I told you, Frank," she ground out, "I'm following up on some leads, but this isn't my story. I'm helping out and I intend to keep helping out. But you are the one choosing what gets printed and what doesn't."

"I waited to give you the chance to make a real splash with this story, to make it known that you've moved from New York to Texas—to our paper."

"I'm making my place," she said. "And it's not in politics. I gave you a good story. Six weeks of a good story with this Marco piece, which you can't deny is doing well."

"Six good weeks," he threw the words back at her. "And then what? You don't have to answer—we both know you don't know. Until you give me a long-term plan that will sell papers, that justifies your salary to my higher-ups, I'll 'justify' for you. Find out why the wife of that soldier visited the mayor," he practically shouted. "Use your connections."

"Frank," she argued. "My father and the mayor represent opposing parties. No one will want to tell me anything." And she didn't want another storm that put her at odds with her family and the media.

"Somebody always wants to talk," he said. "You'll figure it out."

Squeezing her eyes shut, Sabrina accepted defeat. What else could she do? Quit? Then what? "I'll see what I can do," she said noncommittedly.

"I expect to hear a plan of action by Monday." Frank hung up.

Sabrina set the phone down and piled everything back in her purse.

The pizza. She'd forgotten to put it in. She rushed into

the kitchen, eager for any distraction that kept her from calling her parents. Frank had been more than enough trouble on his own. Being busy in the kitchen helped her avoid the call. Ice in cups. Plates. Whoops. Better wipe off the cabinet. She finally gave in and listened to the five messages on her cell from her parents, which sounded about the same as the ones on her answering machine.

It wasn't long before Ryan joined her in the kitchen, allowing her yet another excuse to skip her phone call to her mother. Her career might be in shambles, but she had achieved high merits for procrastination this night, for sure.

"Anything on the messages?" Ryan asked, carrying the pizza to the table while Sabrina grabbed the tea glasses.

"Messages?" she asked, feigning innocence.

He set the pizza in the center of the dark walnut table. "You were going to check your messages and then call your parents."

"Oh, right." She set the glasses down. "Messages. My parents called. Surprise."

"Did you talk to your parents?"

She claimed the seat at the corner. "My boss called and wouldn't let me off the phone. And then I had to make the pizza."

"You had to make the pizza," he repeated, sitting at the end of the table, his scrutiny a bit too earnest for comfort.

"Yes," she said. "And you should eat rather than question me. I slaved in the kitchen."

He studied her a minute more and chuckled. "Slaved, did you? To warm the pizza."

"Are you downplaying my efforts?"

"No. I can't wait to taste your magnificent cooking." He reached for the pizza. "Let's eat." He filled his plate and she did the same.

They'd eaten together, slept together, showered together. And they were going to do it all over again. The idea warmed her and softened the blow of Frank's bullying. *And* of the phone call she couldn't avoid forever. Oh, yeah. And the potential stalker she hoped was no stalker at all.

After a few minutes of debate over the best way to handle her car Monday morning, Ryan reminded her about the front door. "The new key is on the table by the entrance."

"Thank you so much for doing that for me," she said. "I owe you in all kinds of ways."

"You can pay me back by skydiving with me," he suggested playfully.

"Let me think about that," she said, and then immediately followed up with "No."

"One day you'll jump with me," he promised.

"There you go, assuming again," she rebutted.

"Like with the condoms," he said keenly. "The ones we didn't use. I've never been with anyone without using one. I know I said that before, but I want to reiterate that you are safe with me."

Safe. Ryan made her feel safe in ways no other man ever had, yet at the same time, he made her feel as if she were hanging off a ledge by her fingertips—which had nothing to do with condoms. "Me either," she said and then added a reminder, "Though I'm on the pill." She hesitated. "I take it because... It doesn't matter why. You were my first without a condom."

Sexual tension spiked in the air. Something flickered in his face. Satisfaction. Awareness. She felt it, too. They weren't talking about condoms. They were talking about the potential of commitment.

"I like being the first," he said softly and reached for another slice of pizza, breaking the crackling sexual tension down to a mere hum.

They ate and talked, and she couldn't help but catch tiny glimpses of him. He was far more scrumptious than any pizza would ever be. His hair was mussed up, as if he'd run his fingers through it contemplating his task. The day-old beard darkening his jaw, combined with his worn jeans and boots, gave him an appealing, rugged look so much more masculine than the clean-shaven stuffed-shirt types she was used to.

He finished eating and leaned back in his chair, sighing with satisfaction. "Not the best pizza I ever had, but it did the job."

"Hey, now. That's my cooking you're talking about."

"If that's all you can cook, we'll be getting lots of takeout."

Her stomach fluttered at the implication that they'd

be spending time together. "That's generally what I do anyway," she conceded.

He turned serious, shifted the conversation. "So, when are you going to call your parents?"

"Tomorrow," she said. "Today's handed me more than enough trouble as it is."

"Why not get it all over with," he suggested. "Let tomorrow be a new day."

"Maybe. But you heard the message. I'm not sure I'm up to the pressure tonight. They have every intention of coercing me back into politics."

"Which you love," he pointed out, shifting his chair away from the table toward her.

Boots previously disposed of, Sabrina pulled her feet to the chair and angled her body toward him. "I hate politics," she corrected. "I loved exposing corruption and the back-door deals. There's a difference. I convinced myself if I got a big enough audience, I could rally people to stand up for their rights. That's why I encourage voting. We have to speak out in volume. Too many people complain privately, but don't do what they can to speak out."

"And yet you want to walk away?"

She rested her chin on her knees. "I just can't be that person in the middle of all of that conflict anymore," she said. "I can't do any good that way. And I need to feel like I make a difference. Interviewing Marco isn't the way, obviously, but something is out there for me, and it's a stepping stone." She hesitated, wondering about Ryan. "You speak with such pride about the Army," she said. "What happened to make you leave? Because something had to have happened."

"We almost lost one of the Aces while trying to save the young son of one of our third-world allies. We saved the kid, but he never made it to his parents. There had been dealings with an outside agency that was supposed to be on our side, but wasn't. We don't know what happened, but whatever it was, it wasn't right.

"Soldiers take orders without question. Bobby, Caleb and myself all agreed we weren't those soldiers anymore. We were all up for reenlistment within months of each other, and you know the rest. The Hotzone was born. And now, fortunately, I get to lay my head on the same pillow every night. Heck. I have a pillow. There have been plenty of times when that was a luxury."

He said that, and she imagined he meant it—to some degree. But she knew he had to have regrets. Like her, he'd been pushed out of his career, caught in circumstances that he didn't create. "Did you report what happened?"

"We did," Ryan said. "As soon as we were out of the line of fire, wouldn't have been able to have done it any other way. Prosecution followed, but it was all done behind closed doors. Some things are bigger than the people involved. There are unwritten codes, ways soldiers operate to protect the integrity of the organization, and those operating within it. Things best kept between soldiers."

For a flash of a moment, she considered Frank's call. His order that she dig deeper into the story of the soldier and the mayor, and she wondered how Ryan would respond to her doing so. He'd already said he'd like her to stay out of this. All the more reason she had to find a new path for herself. She shook off the thought. Refocused on what felt important to her. Ryan.

"But the Army lost a good soldier fighting for the right values, I don't see how that can be the best outcome."

"Staying wasn't an option," he said, his voice rough with emotion.

Her heart squeezed with his words. Ryan was a hero. The kind of man who really did make a difference. The more she learned about him, the more she wanted to know him. The more she thought this man was *the* man. "Could you have transferred?"

"You don't transfer out of a unit like mine without really good cause. I would have had to explain."

He reached for her and pulled her into his lap. "You trying to get rid of me?"

"Oh, no," she said, her hand settling on his jaw. He smelled so good she wanted to gobble him up. She turned and straddled him, the armless chair giving her plenty of freedom. She twined her fingers around his neck. "In fact, I plan to hold you hostage tonight. In my bedroom."

His hands slid up her back. "Are there any restraints involved?"

She arched over his hips, feeling the thickness of his growing arousal, the heat simmering between them. "I have silk panty hose that might do the job."

"I like silk panty hose," he said. "I think you should go put them on. I'll take them off."

"Why do I get the impression I'm going to be the one ending up in those restraints?"

He nipped her lip. "Because you secretly like giving me control. Admit it."

Her breath lodged in her throat and feathered from her lips. "I'll never admit any such thing." She tried to sound playful, tried to tease him back. But her throat was raspy. Her emotions fluttered in her chest. It was true. She liked giving him control. When she was with Ryan, she liked not having to worry, not having to prove anything to anyone. Ryan made her feel those things. He made her happy.

"I bet I can get you to say it," Ryan vowed. He began to stand, taking her with him.

"Wait," she said, cupping his cheeks. "Are you happy?"

His forehead fell to hers. "I'm about to go make love to you, Sabrina. Of course I'm happy."

It wasn't a real answer. It wasn't the answer she wanted. But he kissed her, a deep, probing kiss that danced along her nerve endings and promised that tonight would, indeed, be happy.

17

SUNDAY MORNING RYAN WOKE to the sweet scent of honeysuckle and the soft warmth of Sabrina's naked body next to his. Beat the hell out of a musty hotel room. Oh, yeah. He could get used to this, and it scared the hell out of him. Nothing in his life was permanent. Sabrina had family and roots, he didn't. He had to keep this real, to remember this was a journey, not a destination.

"Morning," Sabrina murmured, stretching and then rolling to rest her chin on his chest.

"You're awake early," he commented. The sun wasn't even up yet.

"If I am, you are, too," she pointed out.

"I'm fresh out of the Army," he said. "I'm used to early mornings."

"I'll have to break you of that habit."

"You intend to wake up with me often enough to do that, do you?"

She nodded. "I've decided this whole stolen-purse

thing has worked in my favor. You look good in my bed."

He chuckled. "I think the guy is supposed to say that."

"Say it, then," she urged.

"It's not my bed," he said, though he'd like it to be right about now. "But you look good in any bed with me."

She grinned a sleepy grin. "You're such a sweet-talker. How long will I be needing this bodyguard service of yours?"

He rolled her over, slid between her legs. "We'll have to evaluate as we go."

A knock sounded on the door. Ryan arched a brow. "Get many 6:00 a.m. visitors?"

"No," she said. "That's just odd." Alarm slid across her face. "What if something's happened to someone? I should get the door."

Ryan rolled off her and found his pants. "I'll go check it out, so you don't have to get dressed."

She was already getting up, snatching up his shirt. Together they made a complete outfit. "Where's my phone?" She searched the dresser. "Oh. The kitchen."

As Ryan started down the hallway, Sabrina trailed on his heels. "I should have listened to my cell-phone messages," she said. "And I should have called my parents back. What if something is wrong?"

Ryan turned and settled his hands on her shoulders. "Sweetheart. Stop making yourself crazy here. Whatever is at that door, be it a paperboy or bad news, we'll get through it. And they haven't knocked again. It might have been someone at the wrong door."

Her eyes went wide. "Or my mother. She said she'd come here if I didn't call."

"Let's get the door," he said. "Would you like to give me my shirt first?"

She shook her head. "Just open the door! I need to know."

Shirtless didn't seem the way to meet Sabrina's mother, but whatever she wanted. Ryan opened the door. A large envelope fell forward.

"What in the world?" Sabrina asked in astonishment. "Who left me an envelope at six in the morning?"

"I'd wager it's the same person who left your purse."

"Is it safe to open?"

"I guess I'll find out," he said. A few minutes later he had the contents spread out on the dining-room table. Several pictures of a family. One large one of a soldier in full-dress uniform.

"That's the soldier I wrote about," Sabrina said. "Mike Patterson. The one who robbed that bank. How would anyone know to send this to me? I wrote that story under a pen name."

"Obviously someone knows who you are," he said.

Sabrina picked up a picture of a little girl and a boy, elementary-school age. "He had kids. That just breaks my heart." She glanced at Ryan. "Do you think this is the wife?"

"I wouldn't assume anything," he said. "You went to

that news conference. Like Marco's sister Calista, there must have been other people who'd recognize you. My issue here is that this person knows where you live. And it's too much of a coincidence that your purse was stolen. I don't like this one bit."

She hugged herself. "I think I need coffee. Or maybe another margarita."

"What you need is to stay out of this," he said. "Convince whoever this is that you aren't the person to help them."

"Convincing this person might be easier than convincing my boss," she said. "He all but threatened my job last night if I didn't find out why the wife of this soldier visited the mayor a week before he died."

"This could be dangerous territory," Ryan told her.

"What about the kids, Ryan," she argued, holding up the photo. "What if their father wasn't really a criminal? They shouldn't have to grow up believing he was."

He took the picture from her. "Could he have been undercover?" Ryan wondered. "If this soldier was and you expose him as one of the good guys, you may put others in danger. You can't do that. And who knows what the mayor's involvement is, or the wife's. You have to let it go. And if this is the wife, she needs to do the same. She's going to bring attention to herself that she won't like. Just like you will. The truth will eventually come out. You have to figure out a way to make your boss just drop it. This could be a whole different ballgame than what you've dealt with in the past. In fact, we need to think about your safety until this passes."

"I'm not worried about me," she fretted. "It's those kids. I feel bad for them."

"Then make an anonymous donation to them," he said. "I can get you the information to do it. We can organize something for them through the Hotzone, even. Being soldiers ourselves, it would be natural to care for the children of our fallen brothers."

"You'd do that?"

"Hell, yeah, I'd do it, and so would Bobby and Caleb." He drew her hand into his and kissed it. "Come back to bed with me for a while. And I have a good mind to cancel the Realtor today to allow you more time to say thank you."

Back in the bedroom, Ryan sat down on the bed and pulled Sabrina to him, eager to feel her soft skin next to his.

Her hands settled on his shoulders. "House-hunting should be fun," she said. "Why aren't you excited about it?"

"Buying a house is a long-term commitment," he said. "After a lifetime of temporary, I want to get it right. And nothing has felt right."

"What about your family?" she asked. "Where are they?"

"At the Hotzone," he said. "Bobby and Caleb."

"Your real family," she said. "Mother and father."

He'd known this question was coming. Known it and dreaded it. "No family." He wanted to leave it there, but he knew her well enough to know she'd press him, so he added, "My mother dropped me off at a church when I was eight. Said she'd be back, but never returned. I was at an age that adoption was unlikely, so I was moved around from foster home to foster home until I joined the Army."

"So a hotel room, or Army quarters, really is what you see as home," she said, almost to herself.

No. You are, he thought. "It's what I know."

Tenderness filled her eyes and her palm gently caressed his jaw. To his surprise, she offered none of the sympathy he disliked from others. Nor did she immediately speak. She simply stared at him with so much understanding that he could almost have believed that she, too, had no family of her own.

Finally, her lips brushed his, velvety smooth with some unspoken promise, before she stepped back and pulled the shirt over her head. "Cancel the Realtor," she said and slid her arms around his neck. "Stay here with me."

ALMOST A WEEK LATER, on Thursday morning, Ryan pulled into the garage of Sabrina's office building to drop her off at work. Somehow, her car had managed to get front-end damage at the storage facility. A fight with the tow yard had ensued with the yard claiming the car had been damaged before they picked it up. In the end, her car was being repaired and was supposed to be ready that morning. They'd left Sabrina's place, where he'd stayed all week, living a little piece of heaven every morning as he woke by her side at the crack of dawn. But the car wasn't ready, and she'd already turned in her rental car.

"You don't have to wait with me, Ryan," she said. "It'll be an hour until the rental place has a car for me, and it's only a few blocks away."

"But they can't deliver on such short notice," he said. "And I don't want you walking alone."

"You're being paranoid," she said. "I've had a few pictures left at my door. Nothing more."

"Sunday, Monday and Tuesday morning—three packages, left at the door, three days in a row," he corrected.

"But nothing for a couple of days."

"Which means nothing," he argued. "Until we know who is leaving the packages and their intentions, we have to be careful. We assume it's Mike Patterson's wife seeking vindication for her husband. We don't know for sure. Either way, I'm working on the charity foundation for the kids, and we'll take care of them. What their father did or did not become is not their fault. Once the charity is a complete go—which will be in the next day or two—we'll pay their mother a visit. Until then, humor me. I'm having one of those male tough-guy mornings, so go with it."

"You're always having one of those male tough-guy mornings from what I can tell," she commented.

"You'll have to keep me around awhile to make that kind of statement stick."

She cast him a sly look. "Maybe I'll do that."

Man, she knew how to light him up. "Maybe, huh?"

he asked and started to reach for her. She opened the door and slid out of reach.

"Running again?" he challenged.

She peeked in through the door and pursed her lips. "I don't run," she said. "You'll mess up my makeup."

"Sounds fun," he said, thinking of all kinds of wicked ways to achieve that goal.

"Not now, it doesn't," she said. "Not before work. There's a coffee shop a few blocks away. Let's go get a caffeine fix."

He climbed out of the truck and met her at the tailgate. In her light blue suit with a slim-cut shirt and tapered-waist jacket, Sabrina was a better jolt awake than a whole pot of coffee. "Let's skip the coffee and mess up your makeup."

She shoved him playfully. "Behave."

He pulled her close before she could stop him. "You'd rather I didn't."

Glowing, she grabbed his hand and tugged him forward. "Come on. I'm taking you to a public place where I can actually control you."

"Don't count on it." Damn, her backside looked perky and cute in that skirt.

A few minutes later, they sat at a small corner table, nice and close.

"I'll get a rental car, so you don't have to pick me up tonight," she offered, and sipped her caramel macchiato. "I'm meeting Calista for lunch today, too."

"Ah," he said, surprised at this new information.

"Politics just keeps calling. Before you know it, you'll be back in New York, writing for the *Prime*."

Surprise flickered in her face. "You think I'm going back to New York?" She narrowed her gaze on him and seemed to get that he did. "Ryan. I'm not. I like Calista. She called me yesterday and invited me, and I'm glad. I think she and I can be friends. That's part of building a life here. I didn't make the decision to pick up and move here lightly."

"You know she'll try and talk you into speaking at that event again," he warned.

"Because she's passionate about what she does. But that's part of what I like about her." Sabrina's expression darkened, and he could feel her emotionally withdrawing; it was as if the air was being sucked out of the room. Her legs slid away from his.

He reached for her, trying to lean in close. "Whoa. What just happened? Why'd you pull away?"

"Is this… Are you with me because you think I won't be around long? Because I'm temporary? Because, I thought I could do that, I thought I could be that girl, that maybe I wanted to be that girl, but now—" She shook her head. "No, I can't." Resolve thickened her words. "I need to know if you think I'm that girl. If she's who you're after. Because if it is, we need to end this right now."

He'd said to hell with discretion when he'd kissed her on the dance floor, and now he was saying to hell with holding back. He'd never held back in his life. He went for what he wanted. And what he wanted was

Sabrina. "The only way this is temporary is if you make it temporary."

The air thickened with awareness, with emotion. "You scare me, Ryan," she said, her hand covering his.

"You scare me, too, sweetheart," he admitted.

"You think that's normal?"

"Nothing about us is normal," he said. "But maybe that's why it's so good."

"I'm not leaving," she said. "I like it here. But you… you're in that hotel, and it feels like you're one step from rejoining the Army any day."

"Not a chance," he said. "I'm a Hotzone Ace now."

"Then why won't you buy a house?" she said. "And don't tell me you aren't resisting. I've been house-hunting with you."

Ryan had already put himself out there. He was on a roll, and he wasn't going to stop now. "I keep waiting for that feeling of being home I've always imagined I'd feel. And you know the only time I feel it?" His fingers caressed her jaw. "When I'm with you, Sabrina."

She sucked in a breath, her teeth scraping her lip. "You're going to be staying with me the next few days, right?"

"Am I?"

"A good bodyguard would stay with me," she said, "until he was sure the danger had passed."

The danger she didn't think existed. "I believe you make a valid point," he agreed. "I should keep you close. Very close."

"Since we don't know how long this danger might

last," she continued, "it would make sense that you let your hotel go. Save a few dollars while you're staying at my place." She paused and added pointedly, "Until the danger is over."

For just a moment, Ryan went completely, utterly still. Something raw and tender, yet darkly turbulent, spread its fingers inside him. Old memories of the foster home that would be home, but wasn't.

"I need you to call your parents," he said. Her phone sat on the table, next to her purse, and Ryan reached for it.

The tiny smile playing on her lips faded into confusion. "What? Why?"

He settled his head against hers. He'd come this far, he wasn't pulling back. "You say you know what you want," he explained. "Yet you won't talk to your parents, no matter how worried they are. You sent your mother an email. There's something making you avoid them. Something you think they'll trigger. Whatever that may be—if it's going to pull you away from me—as you said, I want to know now."

18

SABRINA STARED AT THE PHONE, before picking it up from the coffee shop's table and slipping it into her purse. "I emailed," she said, making a case to bypass the call. He sat there, his expression indiscernible, and she added, "I'll call. Later." He continued to stare at her, and she continued her excuses. "The car-rental place is about to open. I have to get to work."

Still he said nothing, those somber brown eyes simply assessing her, and she was certain she didn't like the conclusion she felt in them. "You don't understand. This has nothing to do with fear they'll talk me into coming back, or even 'guilt me' into aiding my father's career goals, no matter how grand. I just don't want to listen to them tell me why all my decisions are wrong. I'm free of that. I'm finally doing what I want to do. I'm going after what I want."

"Which is what?" he said, finally speaking.

Which was what? She didn't know and that terrified her almost as much as he did. She didn't know.

Flustered, Sabrina pushed to her feet. "I'll call. Later. But we should go."

They barely spoke on the short walk to the car-rental place, and Sabrina didn't know how to reach out to Ryan. He was like a stranger, shut off and quiet. Her chest began to feel heavy, a flutter of fear inside her. She'd upset him. She had to fix it. By the time they were in the rental car, though, she wasn't sure what to say and he wasn't talking either.

A few minutes later, and only a couple of blocks, she pulled the rental car into the office garage where Ryan had left his truck. "Ryan—"

He popped the door open. "Ask me what I want."

"What?"

"Ask me what I want, Sabrina."

That fluttery horrible feeling expanded, darn near stole her voice, but somehow she did as he requested. "What do you want, Ryan?"

"You," he said. "That's my answer, without any question or hesitation. But it wasn't your answer. You didn't know how to answer. Like I said, I'm good at playing the temporary game, Sabrina, and one of the biggest rules is to walk away if your emotions get involved. So I'm walking away. If you ever figure out what you want, give me a call." He got out and shut the door.

She had sat there for several stunned moments, her eyes burning, when her cell phone rang. Her heart skipped a beat as she scrambled for it, hoping it was Ryan. Without checking caller ID, she answered.

"Where are you?" a male voice asked. It was Frank.

She swallowed against the knot in her throat. "In the parking lot."

"I'll be waiting for you in your office." He hung up.

For an instant, she contemplated driving away. She wasn't up to dealing with Frank. Somehow, she pulled herself together and went upstairs.

As promised, Frank was at her door. He eased back to let her inside. Sabrina set her purse on the desk and pressed her fingers to the steel surface.

All week, he'd pressured her on the mayor's meeting with the wife, and she'd stalled. Given him updates that lead nowhere on purpose, hoping the story would die. But she had to stop playing this game. She had to stop letting everyone push her around.

"We need to talk," came Frank's gruff comment from the doorway.

She shoved the file on her desk to the edge. "You're right. We do. There's your file on the mayor. I'm done. I can do this kind of story in New York."

"I understand you're upset about being exposed, Sabrina," he said. "But the damage is done, and wasn't it inevitable? Take some time to calm down and then let's talk."

"Exposed?" she asked. "What are you talking about?"

Surprised flickered across his gruff features. "You haven't seen the paper?"

"What paper?" Her stomach fluttered with nerves all over again. "What's going on?"

He leaned out the door and yelled. “Kate! Bring me the *Tribune*.”

In a matter of seconds that felt like hours, the paper appeared. Frank flung it on her desk. On the bottom right-hand corner of the front page it read, “With a play for the presidential candidacy expected, did U.S. Senator Jeffery Cameron force his daughter into hiding to silence her challenging rhetoric?”

“‘Challenging rhetoric,’” she muttered in disgust.

Sabrina sat down. Not only had she been found, but her reason for relocating was now all about her father. She was so tired of this kind of mess.

What would Ryan think now?

“I need to go, Frank,” she said, grabbing the paper and her purse.

“What do you mean, *go?*”

“I mean go,” she said. “Now.” He stepped aside.

“As in quitting?”

“I don’t know, Frank.” She passed him and then stopped. Turned back. “Yes. I quit.” Those words felt good. Liberating. She didn’t know what was next, but she knew she didn’t want to do what she was doing anymore. The paper had been the familiar. She’d clung to the past. And it was wrong.

She knew now her future was Ryan. If it wasn’t too late.

She headed down the hallway and Frank called after her, “What about the next installment of the Marco spread?”

She raised her hand. “I’ll call you.”

"Sabrina." Kate, the receptionist, was holding up an envelope as Sabrina passed her desk. "This came for you, marked urgent." It was a white envelope, letter-size, just like the others.

"Thank you," Sabrina said, her chest tight. She darted into the closest restroom and locked the door, then dropped against the wall, letting her purse fall to the floor. Inhaling and exhaling, willing her body to calm. Somehow fighting tears. She didn't want to cry in public.

When finally she could breathe, Sabrina opened the envelope, her hand shaking. There were no pictures. Just a letter.

> I knew who you were the day I saw you at the mayor's press conference, but I had to be sure. That's why I took your purse. To check your ID before I approached you. I intended to return it while you were on the dance floor, of course, but you came back too soon. But either way, I confirmed you were the Sabrina Cameron from New York that I'd read and followed, the Sabrina Cameron who was a champion for the people. Not afraid to go places others wouldn't dare tread. I knew you would help me. I knew you would prove that my husband was innocent. But you didn't help. You were too worried about hiding. You've changed and it saddens me. Well, now you're exposed. You made me tell your secret. My husband was undercover and the mayor was involved. He can clear my husband's

name but he refuses. Now, it's in your hands. Give my kids back their hero. He deserves nothing less than a hero's remembrance.

Sabrina looked for a phone number and found nothing. She had no way to reach this woman. And she had tried to help her, she *wanted* to help her. She should have been faster, dug harder. Involved her father. This was a mess and she felt to blame. Guilt had her back to not breathing, darn near hyperventilating. Suddenly, she felt as if the room was closing in on her. Sabrina yanked open the door and strode to the elevator.

Jennifer was getting off the elevator as Sabrina got on. "Oh, Sabrina. I saw the paper, sweetie. I'm so sorry."

Somehow, Sabrina kept a calm facade. "Can you follow me to my car?"

"Sure."

Thankfully, Jennifer didn't say a word until they were inside the car, as if she knew Sabrina was hanging by a thread. The minute they were inside, though, with the doors shut, the tears came. Jennifer hugged her, a real friend. Something she hadn't ever felt she had. It made her cry more because she knew she'd clung to the past.

Sabrina spilled everything to Jennifer, about Ryan, the letters, everything, but mostly, about Ryan. "So when he asked me what I wanted, I just... I froze. It wasn't that I didn't know I wanted him. I was on the spot. We had been talking about my parents and they'd upset me.

I didn't want to talk to them. I didn't want to feel what they make me feel."

"Did you tell Ryan that?"

"In the wrong way," Sabrina said. "Really wrong way."

"So tell him again. Tell him you want him."

"He isn't going to believe me," she said, swiping at the wetness on her cheeks. She dug a tissue out of her purse. "He won't. Because I didn't say I wanted him first. And now it does look like I want back in politics with that story in the paper today."

Jennifer brushed hair from Sabrina's eyes where it clung to the dampness. "I was afraid for you when you were getting involved with Ryan, because I thought he wasn't capable of falling in love. But I saw him at that bar the night you were in trouble, hovering over you, all puffed up like a protective bull, and I knew I was wrong."

Sabrina blinked through the tears. "You think Ryan is in love with me?"

"Don't you?"

"I don't dare hope right now," she said. "Not after what just happened between us."

"There's only one way to find out," she said. "Tell him you love him. Because we both know you do."

She did but she was scared. "He won't believe me."

Jennifer's eyes twinkled. "I have a plan."

Sabrina wiped away her tears. "But look where your last plan got me."

Jennifer grinned. "Exactly," she said. "Now I have to

get to work but that doesn't mean my *plan* isn't in action." She darted from the car and Sabrina watched her rush toward the elevator. Her friend had filled her with hope. Hope that she could sort this out. Hope that she could make things right with Ryan. Which meant firmly exiting the past. She pulled out her phone and dialed her parents. When she went to Ryan, she was going to be able to tell him that she knew what she wanted. And so did everyone else.

19

RYAN SPENT THE DAY trying not to think about his fight with Sabrina, and failed miserably. By sunset, feeling fouler than a horse with a thorn under its saddle, Ryan concluded a long afternoon in the Hotzone's warehouse, inspecting equipment for the next day. He tossed the final packed chute against a wall with a hard thrust of energy, expelling frustration. Yep. He was just plain foul. In fact, he'd wager to say he downright put the *F* in *foul*.

He hadn't seen or heard squat from Sabrina, which said everything. He'd taken a risk. He'd put himself out there. At least he could say he gave Sabrina everything he had.

Ryan made his way over to the main office, where Bobby jogged toward him. "Hey, man. Jennifer has some emergency at the clinic, and her staff is already gone. I've got a somebody already dressed to drop at sunset that I need you to take."

"What about Caleb?"

"He's got a group of class-B jumpers," he said. "There's no one who can take this one tandem."

Ryan scrubbed his jaw. "Yeah, okay. I'll take the jump. I need to make a quick phone call and I'll be there." The truth was, Ryan had hated the idea of going to that damn hotel again, so he'd called the Realtor for late showings, determined to buy something tonight.

"Great," Bobby said, clamping a hand on Ryan's shoulder. "Head to the training room when you're ready. She'll be waiting there. She wants to learn to jump on her own next time, so we let her sit in on the videos." He took off running.

Ryan cancelled his meeting with the Realtor, and sauntered into the training room of the main building to find it empty. Caleb shoved through the back door.

Ryan held out his hands. "Where's the tandem jumper?"

"In the plane," Caleb said, rushing past him. "I have to make a call."

"In the plane? What's going on, Caleb? You don't leave a tandem alone in the plane." But the other Ace was gone.

Ryan grabbed a chute and the necessary equipment, and headed to the hangar. Well, whoever this jumper was, she'd be getting out of the plane and interviewing with him first. He didn't jump with anyone he thought might freak out in the air.

He entered Hangar One and approached the plane. Joe Cantu, an ex-Army pilot, gave him a salute from behind the controls. Ryan returned the salute and then stepped to the side of the plane. The wind breezed through the hangar door, the scent of honeysuckle blasting him into a dead stop. He inhaled the scent, so familiar, so Sabrina. Then he ground his teeth and silently cursed himself for being such a lovesick puppy over a woman who obviously didn't care about him.

He moved to the edge of the plane and found a petite female inside, facing the wall, her hair tucked into a flight suit, her straps already in place. Customers didn't wear flight suits. That struck him as odd about a moment before a strange, familiar sensation prickled. The scent of honeysuckle once again teased his nostrils, making him abnormally impatient to get his job done for the day. He usually loved jumping.

"Ma'am," he said, climbing into the plane. She was hunched slightly forward, clinging to the side guards. Great. She must be sick. This was going to be quick. They weren't jumping. At least there was a bright spot. "Ma'am. Are you okay?"

The engine started, and Ryan cut his gaze to the front. "What the heck are you doing, Joe? No go! Turn off the plane."

It moved forward. "Joe!" Still it moved. Ryan jerked the door closed, shutting out the force of wind and the noise.

"Ma'am. Are you okay?"

She waved a hand. Enough to let him know she didn't need immediate medical attention, and Ryan headed to the cockpit. They were starting to taxi. "What the hell, Joe?" he demanded, bringing the pilot into view.

"Doing as ordered, boss," he yelled. "Go to the back and enjoy the ride."

Ryan froze, his eyes locked on the front window as they began to lift off. What was going on? And why did he still smell honeysuckle?

He whirled around to the main cabin, and there she was. Sabrina stood there, facing him, her long hair now free around her shoulders, a silky halo that framed her face.

"What are you doing here?"

She moved forward. "Jumping with you."

"No," he said, going to her, settling his hands on her waist. "No, you aren't jumping."

She kissed him. Pressed her lips to his. Ryan tried to resist. No, he didn't. The minute her tongue touched his, he took what she offered and more. He'd thought he could walk away from her, never kiss her again, never feel the delicate, hungry stroke of her tongue against his. And maybe he could, maybe she'd make him, but it would be torture.

A buzzer sounded, the alert telling them they were at jump altitude. Sabrina pulled back. "I want to jump with you. I need to jump with you."

"No," he insisted, noting the way her bottom lip was quivering. "You're terrified."

"I'm with you," she said. "I know I'll be okay. And Bobby showed me everything. I know what to do."

He stared at her, not sure what she was trying to prove. Suddenly angry at the idea that she thought a stunt like jumping out of a plane really solved anything.

Or maybe it did. He was helping her find herself. Wasn't that his job?

He set her back from him and called for Joe to circle one more time. Then went to his knee in front of her, his hands on her knees. "This changes nothing," he said, watching her, his hand sliding up her legs, checking her straps, then ruthlessly brushing the delicate V of her body.

Her lashes fluttered, and he watched the delicate curves of her throat move, but still her chin firmed, stubbornness brimming from her eyes. "You aren't talking me out of this."

He set his jaw and stood, readying their gear, until he stood behind her and pulled her flush against his body, against his hips and the ridge of his cock.

She might have gasped, he didn't know. But her fingers wrapped around his clothing as if she were hanging on for dear life. Instantly, he softened, leaning forward, his lips near her ear. "You're all right. You'll be okay with me." His hands slid down her arms. "Try and relax."

She reached over her shoulder and touched his face. "I trust you."

He felt those words deep inside, inhaled them like he would the air. Jumping out of this plane was huge for Sabrina. In his anger, he'd forgotten just how much so. The buzzer rang again and she tensed. "It's only scary for a few seconds," he promised, and because it was better that she didn't have time to think, he shoved the door open. Wind gusted in at them, Ryan did a quick inspection outside the doorway, and then they tumbled forward.

Her body was stiff, but in a matter of thirty-five seconds, they were under canopy and he knew that the fear would fade. He lifted her arms to the side with his. But she was shaking, not calming down at all. He kept his arms over hers, touching her, something he'd never do with someone else. Tried to point out the lights, the stars, the moon, and finally she relaxed.

Ryan guided them toward a controlled landing in a field, tensed for impact, anticipating confrontation with Sabrina. He wanted this woman, wanted her in a bad way. And he knew how hard it must have been for her to find the courage to jump. There was an obvious message here—she was trying to reach out to him.

But was she willing to give as much as he was—was she willing to give everything? Tension coiled inside him. Fear—unfamiliar, intense. Fear that she was using this jump to tear down his anger, as she'd used excuses to hide from her past. This was a stunt that could have turned deadly.

The landing was smooth, easy, the moon high, the nearby property lights casting them in a visible glow. But there was nothing smooth or easy about what was boiling inside him.

Immediately, Ryan unhooked Sabrina and then cut the canopy, every muscle in his body coiling like the tension in his gut. She crawled forward and pulled off her safety glasses. Jaw set, in pursuit, Ryan followed on hands and knees, catching up with her and turning her over, framing her body with his. His emotions were high. His adrenaline pumping. "What kind of stunt was this, Sabrina?"

She held her chest. "I can't breathe," she heaved. "I can't." She grabbed his arms. "I love you, Ryan."

Stunned, Ryan froze, the air lodged in his lungs. "What did you say?"

"Can't. Breathe. Ryan."

He shook off her words, focused on helping her. "You're hyperventilating," he said, noting her wheezing, her panic. Acting quickly, Ryan sat up and pulled her into his arms. "You're okay." He gently stroked her hair and rocked her. She was pale, her lips trembling. "You're safe. I promise." Rocking with her, he continued to whisper soothing words and slowly her body relaxed. All the while he replayed in his head what she'd said to him. *I love you.*

"Ryan," she whispered, her hand on his chest, turning toward him.

That small sign she'd recovered was all he'd been waiting for. "I love you, too," he said, cradling her face, brushing her lips with his. "More than you can imagine."

A smile touched her face, lighting her eyes. "Even if I never jump again?"

He laughed. "Even if you never jump again."

With their ride back to Hotzone nowhere in sight, he lay down and pulled her to his chest, the stars twinkling above. And that's when she started talking, telling him about the way she'd been outed, and how she'd quit her job.

"So what now?"

"Right before I left New York, some time back, I was approached about writing a book, based on my columns," she said, leaning up on an elbow to look at him. "But I felt I was through then. So I said no. But maybe now. I could focus on a topic that I'm passionate about, and the scrutiny would only come when there was a book release."

"Will that make you happy?"

"You make me happy, Ryan. You're what I want." She inhaled. "I called my parents. I had a heart-to-heart with my father." Her lips lifted. "It was a good talk. He told me I shouldn't let him, or anyone else, bully me into what I write about. He's proud of me. And he said he wants to meet you."

Ryan quirked a brow. "You told him about me."

She nodded. "Yes. I told him about you. I told him I wasn't going anywhere without you, so stop asking. Check out of the hotel, Ryan. Come home with me. *Be* home with me."

The lights of the Hotzone Jeep shone in the distance, and Ryan pulled her close. "I love you, Sabrina," he said. "And I have never felt so at home in my life. *You're* home."

Fifteen minutes later, Ryan and Sabrina walked into the Hotzone training office, with Caleb on their heels. Or so Ryan thought. The door shut behind them.

Sabrina bit her bottom lip and reached for the zipper

on the flight suit. "I thought we might celebrate our newfound love." The zipper slid downward, revealing nothing underneath but a sheer red bra and matching panties.

He was definitely home with Sabrina, wherever she was, wherever they were. Right now, home was the Hotzone training office. And, as it turned out, home was a damn sexy place to be.

Epilogue

A MONTH AFTER HER DARING JUMP from a plane, Sabrina hadn't jumped again. Ryan was still trying to convince her, though. It was Saturday and, to Sabrina's pleasant surprise, one of a number of the new charity days at the Hotzone. There were kids' rides and barbecue, and even a horse or two.

Sabrina stood under the shade of a tree and watched Ricky and Mindy Patterson, ages six and eight, ride one of those horses, their mother, Cheryl, by their side. They were the dead soldier's family. And with the help of the Aces, Cheryl had been convinced that her husband would want her to be safe and accept their help. They'd provided a trust fund for the kids, to which Marco had donated heavily, and so had many others. And the kids had surrogate fathers—three Aces determined to be role models.

There was also skydiving this Saturday, and Sabrina

watched as a plane took off. Her father was inside, about to tandem with Ryan. If that wasn't male bonding, she didn't know what was.

Hours later, when her parents had retired to their hotel room, and the Hotzone was quieting down, Ryan pulled her aside. "I have a surprise. I finally found a home to buy. The Realtor said he could show it to you today."

Sabrina's heart fell to her feet. He was buying a house? Moving out? She'd thought…well, lots of things. Right after accepting the book deal, she'd had an offer to syndicate her column and taken it, hoping it would boost her book sales, ensure her future was filled with choices. Ryan had been supportive.

He kissed her, his eyes twinkling as he led her to the truck. "We need to swing by the condo. I left my checkbook there. If I want the place I've got lined up, I have to act fast." He winked and put the truck in gear. "No more temporary for me."

She tried to smile, but it was hard to work through the swell of turbulence growing inside her. No more temporary for him. Just for her.

"Are you okay?" he asked about halfway to her place, when he couldn't draw her into conversation about her father.

"I think some of the barbecue hit me wrong," she lied.

"Do you want to postpone this?" he asked, concerned. "I can cancel."

"No," she said quickly. "I'm fine." The last thing she wanted was to wait and wonder where this was leading. Which was pretty obvious. Him leaving.

"I'll wait in the truck," she said when they pulled into a space in front of her building.

"Come upstairs," he said. "You can take some meds and lie down a few minutes. We aren't meeting the Realtor for another hour."

Reluctantly she conceded. They exited the elevator, and Sabrina pulled up short. In front of the door was another box.

She grabbed Ryan's arm. "How can this be? Cheryl says she's fine now. She's happy. Surely someone else isn't sending me packages." It was too much on top of Ryan leaving.

"Let's check it out," he said, seeming remarkably calm for someone who prided himself on his "tough-guy protectiveness." He walked toward the box and tugged her with him.

"Hey," she said. "Don't you want to check it out first?"

He eyed the box and then picked it up. "Doesn't look dangerous."

She frowned. He was acting weird. She followed him to the dining-room table, his now infamous potentially-dangerous-package opening center. He pulled a pocket knife out and opened the box lid. "It's for you."

"What if it's dangerous?" Oh, my God. When had he checked out of their relationship so much that he wasn't even worried about her? How could she not have seen it? How could they have made wild, crazy love this morning, and she not sensed the change?

"Fine," she said, hurt expanding inside her. "I'll check it out."

She opened the box lid and removed some papers and frowned when she looked at them. "It's some sort of contract for a home sale." Her eyes went wide as she caught the address. "It's for here." Suddenly, she realized what was happening. "Did you…? Ryan, did you buy this place?"

"I put in an offer," he said. "For us to buy it. Not me. It's not official until we both sign the offer. And a down payment, of course, which I'm prepared to give them today. There's only one thing holding me back."

"What?" she asked, almost afraid to breathe.

"Look in the box."

With an unsteady hand, Sabrina did as he asked. Her fingers brushed a velvet box, and her eyes shot to his. His lit, filling with a combination of excitement and trepidation. She pulled the box out, and he dropped to his knee in front of her.

"It would be my greatest honor if you would be my wife," he said. "I love you, Sabrina. Not only am I not home without you, I'm not alive without you." He popped the lid open to reveal a white diamond that sparkled and gleamed like the hope she'd thought she'd lost not so long ago. She flung her arms around his neck.

"Yes," she said and kissed him. "Yes. Yes. Yes." And then she proceeded to find all kinds of inventive ways to say yes all over again.

* * * * *

COMING NEXT MONTH

Available March 29, 2011

#603 SECOND TIME LUCKY
Spring Break
Debbi Rawlins

#604 HIGHLY CHARGED!
Uniformly Hot!
Joanne Rock

#605 WHAT MIGHT HAVE BEEN
Kira Sinclair

#606 LONG SLOW BURN
Checking E-Males
Isabel Sharpe

#607 SHE WHO DARES, WINS
Candace Havens

#608 CAUGHT ON CAMERA
Meg Maguire

HBCNM0311

Selene wanted nothing to do with the father of her son, Alex; but Aristedes had other plans...that included them.

Read on for an sneak peek from THE SARANTOS SECRET BABY by Olivia Gates, available April 2011, only from Harlequin Desire.

"You were right to turn my marriage offer down," Aristedes said.

And Selene found her voice at last, found the words that would not betray the blow he'd dealt her. "Thanks for letting me know. You didn't have to come all the way here, though. You could have just let it go. I left yesterday with the understanding that this case is closed."

Before the hot needles behind her eyes could dissolve into an unforgivable display of stupidity and weakness, she began to close the door.

The door stopped against an immovable object. His flat palm.

"I can't accept that." His voice was low, leashed.

What did her tormentor mean now? Was he ending one game only to start another?

She raised eyes as bruised as her self-respect to his, found nothing there but solemnity and determination.

Before she could voice her confusion, he elaborated. "I never let anything go unless I'm certain it's unworkable. I realize I made you an unworkable offer, and that's why I'm withdrawing it. I'm here to offer something else. A workability study."

She leaned against the door, thankful for its support and partial shield. "Your son and I are not a business venture you can test for feasibility."

His gaze grew deeper, made her feel as if he was trying to delve into her mind, take control of it. "It's actually the other way around. I'm the one who would be tested."

She shook her head. "Why bother? I know—and *you* know—you're not workable. Not with me."

His spectacular eyebrows lowered over eyes she felt were emitting silver hypnosis. "You're right again. Neither you nor I have any reason to believe that isn't the truth. The only truth. It might be best for both you and Alex to never hear from me again, to forget I exist. But then again, maybe not. I'm only asking for the chance for both of us to find out for certain. You believe I'm unworkable in any personal relationship. I've lived my life based on that belief about myself. I never really had reason to question it. But I have one now. In fact, I have two."

Find out what happens in
THE SARANTOS SECRET BABY by Olivia Gates,
available April 2011, only from Harlequin Desire.

SDEXP0411